WICKHAM'S Diary

AMANDA GRANGE

sourcebooks
landmark

Published by Sourcebooks Landmark, an imprint of Sourcebooks, Inc.
P.O. Box 4410, Naperville, Illinois 60567-4410
(630) 961-3900
FAX: (630) 961-2168
www.sourcebooks.com

Library of Congress Cataloging-in-Publication Data

Grange, Amanda.
  Wickham's diary / by Amanda Grange.
     p. cm.
1. Darcy, Fitzwilliam (Fictitious character)—Fiction. 2. England—
Fiction. 3. England—Social life and customs—18th century—Fiction.
4. Diary fiction. I. Title.
  PR6107.R35W53 2011
  823'.92—dc22
                                        2010049165

Printed and bound in the United States of America
VP 10 9 8 7 6 5 4 3 2 1

WICKHAM'S
Diary

Being an account of his childhood, his
friendship with Fitzwilliam Darcy, and his attempted
elopement with Miss Georgiana Darcy

1784

11th July 1784

Fitzwilliam and I rode out early this morning. We raced down to the river and I won, beating him by a good two lengths, at which I laughed and called him a sluggard. He was annoyed and challenged me to a race back to the house. I accepted the challenge and, once our horses were rested, we set off. He started to pull away from me, jumping the hedge before me, and he reached the drive as I was still crossing the river, so that by the time I reached the stable yard I found him there, waiting for me.

'That is the trouble with you, George, you use up all your energy to begin with instead of holding something back for later!' he said. 'You pushed your horse too hard on the way to the river. He was too tired to give me a race on the way back.'

'Life is for living,' I said with a shrug. 'Live for the moment; win what you can, when you can. There is no use worrying about later.'

Gates, the groom, hobbled towards us and congratulated Fitzwilliam on his victory. I could tell he was pleased that Fitzwilliam had won. It was only right, in Gates's opinion, that Fitzwilliam should be victorious, because Fitzwilliam was the son of Mr Darcy. It reinforced his belief in the scheme of things, that those at the top belonged at the top, and that those beneath them belonged at the bottom.

I dare say I should have believed it, too, if I had been born at the top, but as I have been born at the bottom I think it a stupid arrangement.

Why should I be beneath Fitzwilliam? I am just as handsome as he is; I am just as intelligent, even though he works harder at his books; and I am just as amusing; in fact I dare say I am a great deal more amusing, for Fitzwilliam is so proud he will not take the trouble to entertain other people.

Yet, although he is no better than me, when he grows up he will inherit Pemberley, and I will inherit nothing.

We went into the stables and Fitzwilliam began to tend to his horse. If I were the son of Mr Darcy I would throw the reins to my groom and let him do all the work, but Fitzwilliam always insists on doing it himself, which means that I have to do it, too.

He stood back when he had done it and I could tell that it gave him satisfaction to see his horse well cared for.

Perhaps there is something to breeding after all, for I took no satisfaction in it. I was just relieved to have finished the chore.

Then it was time for us to go home, he to the great house and me to the steward's house.

As we parted at the corner of the drive and I glimpsed Pemberley in all its glory, I thought, One day I am going to live in a house like that, and no humble beginnings are going to stop me.

As I drew near the house I passed a hackney carriage coming the other way and I whooped with delight. Mama was home! I ran in through the front door and hurried into the drawing-room. There was Mama, surrounded by boxes and paper, trying on a new bonnet and admiring herself in the mirror that hung over the mantel-piece, looking very beautiful.

She caught sight of me in the looking glass and spun round, running towards me with her arms wide open and her smile as bright as a flame. If I had been five years old she would have caught me up and spun me round, and I think that for a moment we both of us regretted that I am now twelve and far too old for such things. But she embraced me anyway, and laughed and said, 'Oh, Georgie, I missed you! A week away is too long, but the shops in London! You have never seen anything like them. They are so bright and cheer-ful and full of fine things. And the people! My dear, you have never seen such smartly dressed people in your life. The fashions there are far more advanced than those in the country. There are full skirts and oh! all manner of new things.

I just had to have a few new gowns and I cannot wait to wear them, though what your papa will say, goodness only knows. Well, how do I look? What do you think of my new bonnet? Is it not adorable? Do I not look divine?'

'You look absolutely ravishing,' I said, and it was the truth.

She laughed and said, 'My own darling boy! Now look…' and she ran across the room, throwing open a box and pulling out a coat, spilling paper everywhere. 'I have not forgotten you. I have bought something for you. What do you think of this? Will you not look fine?'

She held it up and I was impatient at once to try it on. It was a red coat made in the hussar style with gold frogging all the way down the front.

'Put it on,' she said.

I threw off my old coat and obliged her, admiring myself in the looking glass, for indeed I did look very fine. She stood behind me, saying, 'You take after my side of the family, Georgie, with your handsome face and your good taste and your love of fine things. You were born to be a gentleman, not the son of a steward.'

'Then why did you marry a steward?' I asked.

She gave a sigh.

'If I had had my way I would have married a wealthy gentleman, but my papa disapproved of him and forbade the match. I was all ready to elope, indeed I had already climbed out of the window, but when I found that the man at the bottom of the ladder was Papa and not Tom, I had to climb back up again. He gave me such a scolding, saying that I was far too young for marriage and that Tom was wild and unreliable, but I was sixteen and ready for adventure and I wanted to go to Scotland with Tom. What fun we would have had! And his grandmama would have come round eventually and then after her death we would have had her fortune and just think what that would have meant to us.'

'I wonder you did not marry him a few years later then.'

'Alas! Tom was indeed wild. His family would not let him see the world so he ran away to sea and was washed overboard in a storm.'

'Why didn't you find another wealthy suitor?' I asked her.

'That is a very sensible question. You are wise beyond your years, George. Of course I would have found another wealthy suitor if I had had the chance, but my papa sent me into the country to stay with my great aunt because he was afraid I would find someone else with whom to elope. Oh, my dear child, I was so bored! There were no shops, no galleries, no theatres; no park to ride in, nowhere to see and be seen; no amusement whatsoever except for the monthly assemblies in the local town, which were as dull as ditchwater. There were no men there under forty there save for your papa.'

'So that is why you married him. I have some-times wondered,' I said, for Mama is like a brightly coloured butterfly and Papa is as sober as a judge.

'That is not the only reason. I also married him because he was a good, sweet darling and utterly devoted to me. And because he had the ear of the greatest man in the neighbourhood, for he had been of some use to Mr Darcy, and I knew that Mr Darcy liked to reward those who had served him well. So I knew that it was only a matter of time until your papa ceased to be a country attorney and became something much better instead. And sure enough, soon after-wards, Mr Darcy made your papa his steward and we came to live here in this dear little house on the Pemberley estate.

'Oh! How happy I was, particularly as I thought it was just the beginning of greater things. But alas! Your papa has no ambition and he was con-tent to remain a steward, looking after another man's property instead of owning his own.

'But you, George, you will rise to greater things. Such a handsome face, together with such charming manners, cannot fail to win you friends in a position to help you. Indeed, you have already made a useful friend in Fitzwilliam, and that friendship will make life easier for you by and by. In fact, it is already making life easier, for what other boy of your age, without wealthy relatives himself, rides the kind of horse you ride and goes to Eton and is free to run around a house like Pemberley? And the friend of Fitzwilliam Darcy will continue to have opportunities that would be denied to a steward's son.'

'Fitzwilliam will go to Cambridge in a few years,' I said. 'And after that, I will seldom see him.'

'My darling boy, you are a great favourite of Mr Darcy's—and how could you not be? You could charm the birds out of the trees—I do not doubt that he will send you to Cambridge with Fitzwilliam when the time comes. Only continue to be charming and respectful and the thing is as good as done. Once there, you will meet a great many useful people, young men from rich families with patronage in all areas of life—although, I cannot see you doing well in a profession, George. No, I think you must cultivate the young men with heiresses for sisters. A life as a gentleman with a rich wife is more suited to you, I think.'

She was distracted by something and, looking over my shoulder, I saw, through the window, that Papa was coming up the drive.

'Now, be off with you, George. Your papa will need careful handling when he sees how much I have spent and I cannot handle him with you here. He will worry too much about setting you a bad example, and he will be embarrassed if I sit on his knee and play with his hair.'

I picked up my old coat and left the room. As I went upstairs I heard Papa come in and go into the drawing-room. His voice floated up to me.

'How many times do I have to tell you that we cannot afford this kind of extravagance?' he asked in exasperation.

I turned round and sat on the stairs so that I could look through the banisters and into the drawing-room. Mama was at her most charming, running towards him very prettily and smoothing his hair back from his face.

'Now, John, you are not to worry; it looks far worse than it is. With the paper all strewn about, and bags and boxes everywhere, it looks as though I have been buying a great deal when in fact I have bought very little and all of it necessary, I do assure you.'

It almost worked. He stroked her cheek, but then he put her away from him and said, 'You must let me know exactly how much you have spent.'

'You surely do not mean me to keep track of every last penny?' she said in astonishment. 'I hope you do not mean to behave like an accountant?'

'My dearest, one of us must. We are not

wealthy, you know. I wish we were, for your sake, but we must take care not to live beyond our income, and that income is not large enough to support your shopping trips.'

Mama tried to distract him, but he would not be fobbed off and at last she had to hand him the bills. He sat down and looked through them and heaved a heavy sigh.

'Darling dear one, don't sigh,' said Mama. 'I have my allowance, you know, and some little money from Mama, and I have not spent so very much more than that, and when you see what I have bought I am sure you will see why I could not leave the things in the shops. I will be very good from now on, I promise you.'

'That is what you said the last time,' he said.

'But this time I mean it,' she said, snuggling onto his lap and stroking his face. 'I do, really, John, I do. I am a trial to you, I know, but I will do better.'

Poor Papa! He never stood a chance!

'You could never be a trial to me,' he said, wrapping his arms around her.

She leant her head on his shoulder, but a minute later she was springing from his knee and saying, 'Then let me show you my new bonnet. You will love it, you know.'

She tried it on and he laughed and said, 'After all, what is the use of a pretty face without a few pretty things from time to time? I can find more work, I am sure. I have time enough. Mr Darcy does not make onerous demands on me, and some of my old clients will hire me to help them with their day-to-day cares.'

Mama kissed him on the cheek, and, having seen enough, I went upstairs where I mused on the fate of Mama and Papa and decided that, when I marry, it will be an heiress. Then I can have all the fine clothes I want, without having to worry about everything I spend.

1788

5th June 1788

Pemberley is full of people this month, for the Darcys have visitors. In general I like it when they have people to stay, for it gives me a chance to practise my charm, but this week's visitors are not to my taste. They are some distant cousins of the Darcys and there is not one daughter amongst the children, but instead there are only sons.

Mama was as disappointed as I was when she found out, for as she said to me, 'You are sixteen now, George, you are of an age to start learning how to make yourself agreeable to girls. You see so few of them, what with being away at school most of the time and then having so little opportunity to meet any through your papa or me, that you must seize every chance you get. And this would have been a good chance. But never mind, make yourself agreeable to the boys, for there is no saying where a friendship with one or another of them might lead.'

I took her advice and I tried to make myself useful. I listened to their tales of hunting exploits and I looked impressed at their stories of romantic conquests, so that I believe the older boys liked me. But the younger boys were more troublesome, particularly as Darcy's parents wanted him to amuse them and of course I had to help him. He brought one of them along when we went fishing this morning. It annoyed me for a moment that he did not ask me if James might join us but then I shrugged, for I cannot expect him to ask me about everything I suppose.

We went down to the river and cast our lines. James did not know how to fish and tangled his line in the bushes and then made a nuisance of himself by fidgeting and saying he was bored. Fitzwilliam told him that he might go back to the house but he shuddered and said that, if he did, his tutor was sure to find him some work to do. He applied himself a little but soon something distracted him, for Georgiana ran down to the river, clutching her doll. She tripped over and dropped it and James, glad of an opportunity to leave off fishing, ran over to her and picked it up. But instead of returning it to her, he held it over her head and laughed as she jumped up and tried to take it.

I could see that Darcy was annoyed.

He said, 'Give it back to her,' but James continued to dance around, waving it over her head.

Georgiana began to cry.

'I said give it back to her,' said Darcy, putting down his fishing rod and going over to James in order to take the doll.

'Make me,' said James, in an infuriating voice.

'I won't tell you again,' said Darcy warningly.

'Good, for I won't listen if you do!' laughed James.

At which Darcy wasted no more words but knocked him down, took the doll, gave it back to Georgiana and then dried her tears. She threw her arms round his neck and gave him a kiss and then ran off to her nurse, who appeared at that moment. The nurse was out of breath, for she had run all the way from the house after Georgiana, but this did not spare her Fitzwilliam's ill humour. He scolded her for letting Georgiana out of her sight, saying that if he had not been by the river then his sister could have fallen in. The nurse looked abashed and hid her novel behind her back so that he should not see the reason for her negligence. She apologised and then she took Georgiana by the hand and retreated with her charge in tow.

We settled down to our fishing again. James had picked himself up and was much better behaved to Darcy. He had a bruise coming up on his cheek, but he said no more of being bored and tried to do as he was told, ending the morning by catching two very fine fish.

'So Fitzwilliam is giving orders already, is he?' asked Mama, when I told her of the incident.

'He has the natural Darcy authority. Study him, George. That authority will be useful to you in the future.'

'Mama, you know I have no authority!' I said with a laugh. 'I cannot give orders for the world! Anyway, why should I need to? As you are so fond of telling me, I have charm!'

'Impudent boy!' she said, ruffling my hair affectionately. But then she became more serious. 'Charm is a great asset in life, but there are certain people who will not respond to it at all. Amongst them are tailors, bootmakers, and tradespeople, people you will need to converse with in the future. They will grant long credit to a man who behaves as though he owns the world, but they will not give anything to a charming rogue, for they know that charm never paid a bill. You must study people carefully, George, so that you can decide which manner will best suit the people you are dealing with. Sometimes charm and sometimes authority. Try it now.

Stand up very straight and look down your nose at me. Just think of Fitzwilliam. He has the true Darcy spirit. There is not a tradesman in the land who would refuse him credit, though he is only sixteen years old.'

I tried to assume Darcy's posture and expression, and Mama laughed and said that I did it very well, at which I collapsed into laughter beside her.

'I wish I were Fitzwilliam,' I said, when we had recovered. 'Then other people would have to study how to please me, instead of me studying how to please them.'

'My dear George, you would hate it if you were Fitzwilliam. He will grow up to inherit a lot of responsibility as well as his money, something you would not like at all. You are better as you are.'

I thought there was something in what she said. Even so, I would happily change places with Fitzwilliam. Then I could pay someone to take care of my responsibilities and I could spend my time enjoying myself.

8th June 1788

The morning was hot and Fitzwilliam and I escaped from the schoolroom and ran down to the river, where we dived in and swam to our heart's content.

'I love Pemberley,' he said, as he swam lazily on his back, looking at the sky, which was a clear and cloudless blue. 'I could not be happier, knowing that one day it will all be mine. Do you love it, too?'

'Of course I do,' I said, thinking, One day, when I marry an heiress, I shall have an estate just like it.

'Do you think you will be the steward here, after your father?' he asked.

His words shattered my daydream. He saw me, not as a landowner and an equal, but as a steward, someone who would spend the rest of my life serving him. I felt myself grow red with anger and mortification, but, remembering Mama's advice, I thought of a way I could turn the situation to my advantage.

'To do so I would need a good education,' I said. 'Papa went to university, you know, courtesy of a kind uncle, but I have no such relative to sponsor me.'

'As to that, I believe Papa means to send you to Cambridge with me. He thinks a great deal of your papa, you know, and he wants to help you because of it.'

'I had never imagined… that is very kind of him… I will try to be worthy of him,' I said, expressing myself surprised and suitably grateful.

Fitzwilliam smiled and said, 'I am glad we will be there together. It will be good to have someone there I know. All my cousins are the wrong age to be there with me, either just too old or just too young.'

I tried to think of Fitzwilliam at Cambridge and I wondered what he would do there, how he would comport himself. He would be unconsciously arrogant, no doubt, behaving as though he owned the place.

Such behaviour would not do for me. I would have to follow Mama's advice. I would make friends, meet their sisters, and marry an heiress.

When I returned home, Mama was very pleased to hear that Mr Darcy meant to send me to Cambridge, and she laughed when I said I meant to take her advice.

'A wise decision. You do not have the temperament to apply yourself to the books, Georgie, and you certainly do not have the temperament to be poor. You have winning manners and good looks and they will be a great help to you. But, whilst you should spend most of your time trying to hear of any suitable heiresses, you should not neglect any other opportunities that might come your way. You might have to wait a few years for the right heiress to come along. In the meantime, there are some valuable livings hereabouts. If you continue to win Mr Darcy's approval, then he might give you one of them when you grow up.'

'A living? What, as a churchman? Mama! You are joking? I have no desire to go into the church.'

'Why not? It will give you a gentleman's residence and a good income, for which you need do very little work. You need only look the gentleman, which you can do very easily, and hire a curate to write your sermons for you. You will have an entrée into all the best society and you will meet many sheltered young ladies who do not go out a great deal in the normal way. Moreover, they will already be disposed to like you, for you will appear to great advantage in the pulpit, and do not forget that you will not have any competition in church, as you would at a ball. A clergyman is the king in his own church. He reigns supreme.'

I thought about what she said, and I remembered that I had noticed the girls casting lingering looks at the Rev Mr Mathias last Sunday, despite his plain looks.

'I think, perhaps, it might be a good idea,' I said. 'I could wear a black suit and have one simple pin—a diamond—in my cravat.'

I thought of myself standing in the pulpit, with everyone admiring me in my new black suit, and all the girls swooning over me, and I thought it would do very well, at least until I found my heiress.

'Then set your sights on the church, George, and on the rich living of Pemberley. The parsonage is a fine house, far better than this one, and it is capable of further improvement. It is well situated, and it would not shame a far wealthier man than you. And why not set your sights on Georgiana Darcy, too?'

'Georgie? She is little more than a baby!' I said, laughing at the thought of it.

'But she will not always be so. Little children have a habit of growing up, you know, and there is not such a great difference in age between you. When she is ready for marriage you will not yet be thirty. And she has a handsome dowry, thirty thousand pounds.'

'That is so,' I said thoughtfully.

'A man can go far with thirty thousand pounds. He can take a house in town for the Season, and better yet, as the husband of Georgiana Darcy, he will be admitted into the highest society, for do not forget that her uncle is an earl. And the beauty of it is that no one will blame you for mixing so much in the world, as they might do if you did not have such an exalted wife, for you can say that you are doing it for her sake and not your own.'

'And we can go to Brighton in the summer, and Bath in the autumn,' I said, seeing a happy future stretching out in front of me.

'You can indeed. You can travel as much as you desire.'

'Though it is a long time to wait,' I said, feeling suddenly dissatisfied. 'I do not think it will suit me to live on a narrow income until I am thirty. I would rather have my heiress sooner.'

She smiled at me.

'You have your mother's impatience, alas! Very well, what about Anne de Bourgh? She is coming here next week. She is another wealthy heiress; indeed, she will be richer than Georgiana, for she will inherit Rosings Park. Should you like to live there, George?'

I was much struck by the idea.

'I have never been, but it sounds very grand,' I said, adding, 'far better than a parsonage.'

'You are right, it is a great house, a very great house, with an extensive park and delightful gardens. It is in a delightful part of the country, too, being in Kent, and so very convenient for London. I went there once when I was a girl. Oh, not to stay, but just to look around when the family was away. I was touring the area with Mama and Papa, and Mama had a wish to see it. If an opportunity arises for you to visit it, you should not neglect it. I think you would like Rosings very well.'

'And no doubt you would like it very well, too!'

'I cannot deny that I would welcome a suite of rooms there,' she said with a dimple. 'You must not forget your mama when you are well settled.'

'I will never forget you. I will give you an allowance and you may shop to your heart's content.' My mood sobered. 'But it is out of the question,' I said, abandoning the rosy picture reluctantly. 'Anne is intended for Fitzwilliam. I heard Lady Anne and Lady Catherine talking about it the last time the de Bourghs were here. They want their children to marry, indeed they have been planning it since Fitzwilliam and Anne were in their cradles.'

'They might intend Anne for Fitzwilliam, and they might have no difficulty in getting her to agree to the match, but I think they will find it hard to get Fitzwilliam to fall in with their plans. He has no inclination for Anne. I have watched them together, and although he is always polite to her, he never chooses to spend any time in her company and he says barely two words to her beyond what is necessary. There are some boys who could be encouraged into such a match but I do not believe that Fitzwilliam is one of them. There is a strength about his character, something that will not be encouraged or bullied or coerced. He knows his own mind and he can be firm to the point of stubbornness when he believes himself to be right. He will marry to please himself, you will see, like his mother and his aunt. They both made love matches and I believe that Fitzwilliam will do the same.'

'I did not know they made love matches,' I said, startled, for both ladies married very well.

'Oh, yes, it was something of a scandal at the time. Lady Anne was destined for much higher things. She was the daughter of an earl, you know, and her father wanted her to marry a title, but she met Mr Darcy at a ball and from then on she would countenance no one else. Her father tried to persuade her by appealing to her vanity, telling her she could marry an earl, but she said she already had her own title and did not need another one. Mr Darcy was very handsome, of course, and he had an air about him—Fitzwilliam has it, too—something challenging, something that is very appealing to women. Her father railed at her, telling her that she was descended from William the Conqueror; for, you know, Fitzwilliam means the son of William and it implies royal blood.'

'How so?' I asked.

'Kings have a habit of adding Fitz to their own name when they christen any children they might have with their mistresses, instead of with their wives. But Lady Anne only retorted that the name of Darcy would not shame anyone, and she called her son Fitzwilliam Darcy to prove it.

'Lady Catherine was just as headstrong.

'They were the rage of the Season, those

two girls, Lady Anne and Lady Catherine. Lady Anne was the pretty one but Lady Catherine had something in her air and manner which set her apart. Sir Lewis de Bourgh fell under her spell as soon as he saw her, though it is less certain what she saw in him. An easygoing temperament, perhaps, a man who would allow her to mould him. But whatever the case, there was a great deal of love on both sides.'

'I cannot imagine Lady Catherine being in love,' I said thoughtfully.

'She has grown colder since Sir Lewis died. And Anne has grown colder, too. She used to be much happier, poor child. I think she would make you a very good wife. She would be easy to mould, like her father, and she would be grateful for your attentions. She is a plain little thing, and a handsome boy like you who is respectful and friendly and who can make her laugh is sure to have a chance of winning her affections. Play with her, George, dance with her—little girls always like someone to dance with them, and she is too old to be climbing trees with you now—talk to her, draw her out, be a friend to her, flatter her, look at her as though she is the most important person alive. You are so young that Lady Catherine will not be on her guard, as she will be when Anne is of a marriageable age, and such kindnesses now might well pay dividends in the future, for Anne is sure to remember them.'

'Very well, I will dance with her, I promise you, and be kind to her and amuse her.'

The more I thought of the idea, the more I liked it.

George Wickham, rector of Pemberley, would be somebody, certainly. But not nearly as great a somebody as George Wickham, master of Rosings Park.

15th June 1788

The de Bourghs have arrived. The day being wet, Fitzwilliam and I were playing at billiards and so I was at the house when the carriage rolled up the drive. The de Bourghs went to their rooms to rest after their journey, but they soon joined the Darcys in the drawing-room and one of the servants came to request the presence of Fitzwilliam. I followed him quietly, effacing myself so that no one should notice me, and I watched him as he greeted his father's guests. He was polite to Anne, but nothing more. He asked after her journey and said that he hoped it had not tired her, but then he retreated into his customary hauteur and said no more, unless Lady Catherine directed a question at him.

I went quietly over to Anne, without drawing attention to myself. I asked her about her journey and made a few remarks on the weather, then I pulled the screen forward to protect her from draughts—and to hide myself from other eyes: if they had noticed me they might have expected me to leave. I made myself agreeable to her, and she soon began to smile and then to laugh. She is really not so plain when she laughs. I found her easy company, expecting nothing, but taking a shy pleasure in my company and in my compliments. Poor girl! I think she has little enough attention from anyone else, unless it is to fuss over her health. I think I could do her good if I were her husband. I would amuse her and entertain her and make her happy, and in return I would have the position I deserve. I think I should like being married to Anne.

18th June 1788

Mama was right; Lady Catherine does not consider me a threat and she smiles on my attentions to her daughter, seeing them as Miss Anne de Bourgh's due. I overheard her remarking to Mr Darcy that I had excellent manners and saying that I would make a good courtier.

I wonder... George Wickham, courtier. George Wickham, knight.

If I was a knight I would be *Sir* George Wickham... Sir George Wickham of Rosings.

Yes, I like that very well.

24th June 1788

Another wet day. After we had finished our lessons, Fitzwilliam and I were called into the drawing-room to entertain Anne. Fitzwilliam made a few cursory remarks and then fell silent, being in a restless mood. I could tell that he was longing to be out of doors, for he does not like to be confined, and wet days are a hardship for him. His restlessness made him more brusque than usual and, when Anne ventured to say that it looked as though it would rain all day, he was curt with her. She was downcast, but I soon lifted her spirits by saying that we must have some exercise and that, even though it was raining, we could dance. Her mother overheard me and said that it was a good idea, for Anne was an accomplished dancer. She then instructed Anne's companion to play the piano. I made Anne a courtly bow and asked her for the honour. She blushed, but she took my hand readily enough and I led her out into the middle of the room. I took care not to dance too well, for I know that Lady Catherine likes rank to be preserved and I did not want to outshine her daughter. But I danced well enough to show Anne to advantage, covering for her small mistakes. Anne herself enjoyed dancing with me. Her face was flushed, and she looked sorry when the dance was over.

Lady Catherine then said that Fitzwilliam should dance with Anne. Poor Anne! Her face fell, and she watched him walking towards her with trepidation.

Fitzwilliam was scarcely any more pleased, for he is not used to falling in with the wishes of others, but he could not refuse. He took her hand reluctantly and danced well, but I believe that Anne enjoyed dancing with me more.

Lady Catherine was so well pleased with the afternoon that she suggested the Darcys hold a party 'for the young people' and that after a light meal there should be dancing.

'It is time for Anne and Fitzwilliam to learn how to go on in public,' she said. Then, addressing Fitzwilliam, she said, 'You bear a great name, Fitzwilliam, and you must not disgrace it.'

The party was agreed upon, and when I returned home I told Mama all about it.

She clapped her hands in glee and said, 'Excellent, George! This is just the kind of opportunity you need. You will have a chance to meet all the neighbouring heiresses and to impress them with your charm and good manners. Any friendships started now may well be continued, if circumstances are favourable, when you are of marriageable age. You will be able to bring yourself to their notice if you should meet them out in the world, for you will be acquainted. You can give them news of the Darcys and, the conversation being thus begun, you will know how to continue it. This party could be the start of great things for you. Now, we must look through your clothes and decide what you are going to wear.'

30th June 1788

I arrived at Pemberley in good time for the party and I had the good fortune to pick up a handkerchief that a girl had dropped, later to discover that she was a Miss Layson and that she would have ten thousand pounds when she came of age.

I spoke to her again when I met her in the drawing-room, and she was friendly towards me. I bowed and moved on, and I was just congratulating myself on making such a useful acquaintance when I heard her friend sniggering behind my back. I could not hear what she said, but the words, 'only invited because they were a boy short' reached my ears. Mama had warned me that I would hear this kind of thing and that I must not mind it and so I took no notice, but set out to please each and every one of the girls present.

I did not neglect Anne, either, and I danced

three times with her. She knew the first dance well enough but in the other two she was forever going wrong. Unlike the other boys I did not shout at her, I set her right kindly. At the end of the dance I told her that she danced well, for superior dancing consisted not only of performing the right steps but of dancing with elegance and grace. She smiled up at me shyly and I thought of the day when she and I would be opening the dancing at Rosings together as Mr and Mrs Wickham. This thought brought a smile to my face. But as I led her back to her mama I heard a snigger of 'steward's son' coming form the girl who had laughed at me earlier. I was for a moment perturbed, but Anne squeezed my hand and said, 'Ignore her, George. Melissa Harbridge has always been mean, and anyway she has no right to say such things, because her grandfather was only a blacksmith.'

I thought then that Melissa had done me a service, for she had won Anne's sympathy for me.

I continued to make myself agreeable to every-one at the party and I went home well pleased.

Mama was eager to hear all about it. At the end of my recital, she said, 'Well done, George. We will have you at Rosings, just you see!'

7th July 1788

The de Bourghs left this morning. I managed to see Anne before she departed, for I knew she would be taking a walk through the rose garden. I pretended that I had met her there by accident and, as I walked along beside her, I told her how much I had enjoyed her visit and that I hoped to see her again before very long. She said that her mama had no plans to visit Pemberley again for the time being, and that the Darcys would visit Rosings next.

I asked her about Rosings, saying, 'Is it as big as Pemberley?' to which she replied, 'Oh, yes, it is just as big and just as fine. The gardens are bet–ter, for Papa liked flowers and so they are always very colourful. The Rosings park is also, I think, more beautiful.'

'Shall you like to inherit it, or will it be a burden to you?' I said.

'I shall like it, I think. It means I will never have to leave, not even when I marry and I do not think it will be difficult to care for because I will have a husband to help me look after it.'

'Then let us hope he knows how to care for an estate,' I said, thinking that the fact of my father's stewardship might be of some advantage to me after all.

'I think he will,' she replied.

And I wondered, Is she thinking of me?

She smiled at me and I smiled in return.

Perhaps she was making no more than a general remark, but even so, as I stood at the corner of the drive this afternoon and waved to her as she passed by in her carriage, I felt I had made the most of my opportunity, and when she waved back I went inside feeling well pleased.

10th July 1788

Papa took me round the estate with him this morning and I paid attention to everything he said. I took a new interest in it. I might need to know how to run an estate, not as a steward, but as a landowner. Even if I do not marry Anne, I will surely marry an heiress, and one day I will have my own estate to care for.

16th July 1788

Lady Anne's brother and his family have arrived. Mama was very excited when they arrived, for Lady Anne's brother is an earl and his coat of arms was emblazoned on the side of the coach. His footmen wore livery and so did the coachman. The whole procession made a splendid sight.

'Henry is about your age,' she said to me as she turned away from the window. 'I want you to make friends with him if you can, George. He is interested in soldiering and he intends to go into the army. If you pretend an interest in the army, too, then perhaps he will invite you to stay when the Darcys go to visit him and his family.'

I pulled a face at this, for I have no interest in the army, and I knew it would be difficult to find something to say to a boy who was determined to become a soldier, but I promised to try.

I went down to the river, knowing that Fitzwilliam intended to take his cousin there, and I was soon one of the party. There were some other boys there, too, and I made the most of the opportunity. I worked my way round next to Henry and introduced the subject of the army, but as it soon became apparent that I knew nothing about the life of a soldier, I thought it would be better not to pretend any longer, so instead I was honest and said that the life would not suit me. Not willing to waste an opportunity, however, I said that I would prefer to go into the church. He did not seem to be interested, and he did not say anything about his family's livings, as I had hoped he might, but there must be some, and when the time comes, perhaps my words might bear fruit.

20th July 1788

I was practising my dancing steps with Mama this afternoon when Papa came in and said that Mr Darcy wanted to see me. Mama said that I must put on my best coat and change my cravat, and once that was done I set out for the great house.

I was shown in at once and Mr Darcy smiled at me and said that I should sit down. Then he said, 'I understand that you have some thought of going into the church when you are a man.'

'Yes, sir,' I said.

'Do you believe you could deliver good sermons?' he said.

'Yes, sir, I do.'

He nodded and said, 'So do I. You have always had a clear speaking voice, George. It is pleasant to listen to and it carries well. Your masters tell me you have some oratory skills and that you have the ability to sway your listeners. You know, of course, that there is more to being a clergyman than giving sermons?'

'Yes, sir. A clergyman is responsible for his parish and his parishioners. He must set them a good example and help them with their daily life as well as officiating at the usual ceremonies. I think I could do that, sir.'

He looked at me intently and then he said, 'I believe you could. I have watched you a great deal lately, George, and what I have seen has pleased me, for I have seen that you care about people. I noticed you trying to please Anne when she was here, and that was good of you, because, as you know, she has been in low spirits since she lost her father. Then, too, you have always been kind to Georgiana. It is not every boy who would take the trouble to speak to a little girl and show an interest in her early attempts at needlework and other accomplishments, as I have seen you do. And I noticed you on the lawn a few weeks ago, helping her to learn to dance.

'It is early days yet, you are still very young, but if you are of the same mind in a few years time, I will give you the means to train for the church. Once ordained, I will make one of the family livings available to you. The one at Church Cross will probably suit you, and if you do well there, I have other livings in my gift which will be yours in due course.'

I expressed myself surprised and grateful at his interest in my future. He smiled and said that he had always been pleased with my father's stewardship and that he liked to reward those who served him well.

And there it was again, that word *serve*.

I hid my feelings, thanked him again for his words, and left his study. I went straight home, where I told my parents what had happened.

Papa was very pleased and so was Mama. In

truth, I might do a great deal worse, but then again I might do a great deal better.

Both Anne and Georgiana like and trust me. Who knows what the future might bring?

1790

25th September 1790

Papa lectured me this morning on the many pitfalls awaiting a young man on his going to university, the bad crowds he might fall in with, and the perils of gambling, drunkenness, and licentiousness. I listened with an interested air, but underneath I could not wait to be gone. Only think, two more weeks and I will be in Cambridge, with all the bustle, noise, and buildings; the air of wealth and importance; the fashionable vehicles and the finely dressed people!

'This is your chance,' said Mama to me this afternoon. 'Make good friends, George, friends who can help you. You will need to drink with them and gamble with them but keep your wits about you. Never play cards when you are drunk and never compromise a young lady who has relatives to support her. Stick to women of the lower orders, pay them for their services, make yourself agreeable to anyone with wealthy sisters, and you should do well.'

'I mean to, Mama. And when I have caught an heiress I will take you to London and you can shop to your heart's content.'

'I am too old to think of shopping now,' she said with a sigh.

'Nonsense, you are the prettiest woman in the neighbourhood even now, and I'll warrant the prettiest in the country as well.'

She laughed, and I bowed and she curtseyed, and then she went to her escritoire and took out a purse. She opened it and I saw that it was full of money.

'How did you come by such a large amount?' I asked her in amazement.

'I have been saving it for you,' she said.

'Saving?' I asked incredulously.

'My dear boy, see how I love you. I would even save for you! I knew your papa would not give you enough money to go away with and so here is some more. Spend it wisely. Throw some away to begin with—you are young and you need your fun like everyone else—but then think how best to spend it because it will not last forever. Clothes are important; they will mark you out as a gentleman, and, moreover, a gentleman of the right sort. See what the other well-bred young men are wearing and do likewise. Go to their tailors. Show them that you are one of them, and everything else will follow: invitations to country estates, dinner parties, balls, and all with the best families. Be friendly and open, but not too open: there is no need to mention what your father does for a living. If you are asked, it is enough to say that he is a gentleman.'

I took the money and put it in my portmanteau, ready for the day when I will go to Cambridge. Then I went out to the stables because the weather was fine and I was in need of some exercise, and I found Fitzwilliam there.

He has grown lately and he is now several

inches taller than I am. It makes him look even more proud, for he holds himself well, and there is an air of being *someone* about him that I cannot match, no matter how hard I try.

Whenever we go to private balls he is always the centre of attention, even though he is only eighteen. I wish I could think that it is just because of Pemberley, but there is something else that attracts people to him. It is not charm. I have charm, which means that people are always pleased to talk to me and to dance with me whenever I ask them. But they would rather dance with Darcy. Their eyes follow him, even though he makes no effort to please them, for he is often bored and he does not trouble to disguise it. He walks about the room as though he wants to be somewhere else—anywhere else—and he will only dance if he is introduced to his partner in such a way that he cannot avoid it. He never puts himself out to please, as I do.

As I must.

'Where shall we go?' he asked, as he mounted his animal and waited for me to saddle my horse.

I was pleased that he wanted my company, for I do not spend as much time with him as I used to.

'Down to the river,' I said.

He turned his horse's head and then he set off, leaving me to catch him.

'Are you looking forward to going to Cambridge?' I asked him as I drew level with him at the ford.

'Looking forward to it?' he asked. 'What has that to do with anything? I am of an age to go to Cambridge, and so to Cambridge I must go.'

'Do you not want to go?' I asked in surprise.

He looked into the distance, at a spot on the horizon, but when I followed his gaze, nothing was there, and I had a feeling that he was looking inwards and not outwards.

'Sometimes I do not know what I want,' he said.

There was an air of restlessness and dissatisfaction about him and I looked at him curiously.

'I thought you were happy to be a Darcy of Pemberley.'

He brought his eyes away from the distance and fixed them on me.

'And so I am. But there is something missing, George. Do you not feel it?' he asked, searching my gaze.

Yes, I thought, there is something missing. A large estate and larger fortune. But I did not say it.

And besides, those things were not missing for him.

'No,' I lied.

He looked away, over the estate.

'There are no surprises in my life. It is all mapped out for me. Eton, Cambridge, marriage to some suitable heiress, an heir…'

'If all you want is surprise…' I said, and throwing myself off my horse and into the river, I caught hold of him and pulled him in, too.

He emerged, splashing and choking, a minute later, and for a moment I did not know if he would shout at me or laugh with me. I saw the boy inside him warring with the man he was becoming and for a moment I was not sure what the outcome would be, but then he laughed and ducked me and we emerged, dripping wet, and lay on the bank in the sun for our clothes to dry.

1791

25th January 1791

It is a relief to be in Cambridge and away from the watchful eyes at home. There were one or two incidents with milkmaids and tavern wenches over the Christmas holiday, enjoyable in themselves, which nevertheless started rumours about me. Once or twice I thought I caught old Mr Darcy looking at me speculatively, as though he might have heard them. He is such a paragon of virtue himself that he disapproves of such behaviour in others, and Fitzwilliam is almost as bad. He thinks the master of the manor should be careful not to take advantage of his situation— although I suspect that he has a little opera dancer tucked away somewhere, for he visits a certain area of London more often than is necessary for a man in his position.

And that is the thing about Fitzwilliam: he now seems like a man, whilst I still feel like a boy. I still see him, though, and we still get on well enough when we are together, which is fortunate, because it allows me to find out what is happening to Anne de Bourgh. Fitzwilliam talks about her with little interest, and I believe that Mama was right, he will not marry her. And if he does not, someone else will, and why should that someone not be me?

10th February 1791

Mama wanted to know all about my friends at Cambridge when I went home for a few days. I was surprised to find her unwell, but as she lay on the sofa, I told her about the men of all types, the hard-riding countrymen with their well-worn boots and ill-fitting coats; the studious men with their abstracted air and their boots on the wrong feet; the wild men with their whoops and their drunkenness; and the dandies in their breeches that never wrinkle and their diamond tiepins.

She asked me about Fitzwilliam, and if I was still friends with him, and what he did at Cambridge. I told her that he was aloof, that he did not mix freely with the other men, that he had no taste for the drunks or the countrymen, and that he was unimpressed with the dandies' wealth. Mama said that she was not surprised, for he has seen far more ostentation at Leighford

Castle, where he goes to stay with his Fitzwilliam cousins, than even Cambridge can muster.

I have never been invited there, despite my best efforts, but I live in hope that I may one day cross the threshold. There are two daughters, both unmarried, and although their parents would not approve of me as a son-in-law, the daughters are, by all accounts, headstrong. And when has a parents' disapproval ever stopped a headstrong girl from doing anything?

14th February 1791

Fitzwilliam came to my lodgings this evening. He was bored, and he strode around the room like a tiger in a cage. I said as much and he turned to me and said, 'Do you ever feel you are looking for something, George?'

A rich wife, I thought, but I did not say it. It would not do to let Fitzwilliam know that I am hoping for an heiress, or he might think to keep Anne and Georgiana away from me. And he would definitely not persuade his cousins invite me to Leighford Castle.

'No,' I said. 'Do you?'

He drummed his fingers on the mantelpiece. 'Yes.'

'What?' I asked.

'I do not know,' he said with a frown. 'But I will know when I find it.' He was thoughtful for a while and then he said, 'Let us go out.'

'Where?'

'To my club.'

'I am not a member.'

'That can easily be remedied,' he said. 'My name will be enough to have you elected.'

We went out together and I soon found myself in a respectable establishment, too respectable for my tastes, though not for my purposes. I looked around me, making a note of names and faces, for who knows when the men at the club might prove useful in some way?

Fitzwilliam was still restless. He talked of his mother's devotion, his father's belief in him, his hopes for Cambridge, and his plans for the London house, but his mind was on none of it.

He knew everyone at the club and he introduced me. Before long we were talking to half a dozen fellows of our own age and we were soon on our way to a party organised by one of them.

When we arrived, I saw the way the women looked at Fitzwilliam and I thought, my mother was right, there is something about him that women find a challenge.

But then I thought no more of Fitzwilliam, for we soon became separated and not all of the women wanted a challenge. Some of them wanted a man to tease them and flirt with them and I was happy to oblige them.

16th February 1791

I found myself drinking with Peter de Quincy tonight. I have seen him often before and exchanged a few words, but this time we spent all the evening together. He is a man after my own heart, though fortunately not a man after my own pocket. He is very wealthy, has a taste for drink and women, and his money is so easily come by that he can afford to give it away to friends who amuse him. He has recommended me to his tailor and he has given the man instructions that everything is to be put on his bill.

'There isn't a man in Cambridge can wear a coat like you do, George,' he said. 'And if there's one thing I want from my friends, it's that they don't disgrace me. We're going to a party at old Geffers's rooms tomorrow. You'll like old Geffers and you'll like his company more. He has a way of finding the prettiest and the most willing women in any city he's staying in, and his cellar's the best you'll find anywhere in the county.'

18th February 1791

We had a riotous night last night and I was just returning to my own room at seven o'clock this morning when I saw Darcy. He was up early and going out for a morning ride.

'Join me,' he said.

'My dear fellow, I am in no state for a ride.'

He eyed me distastefully.

'So I see. If you must drink, George, do it in better company. De Quincy has a bad reputation.'

'Are you afraid he'll lead me astray?' I asked, laughing.

'Yes, I am,' he said seriously. 'It's easy to get into bad habits somewhere like this, where there is no regular life to drag you out of them.'

'Good God, Darcy, you sound like my father!' I said.

'Will you come with me, George? The fresh air will do you good.'

For a moment I wavered. The thought of riding through the early morning countryside had a certain appeal. But my head hurt and in the end I declined. There will be time enough for riding in the holidays when I am back at Pemberley. I mean to enjoy myself whilst I am at Cambridge.

6th March 1791

Damn! My head hurts. I wish I could remember
what I was doing last night, where I went and who
I was with. What was it that Mama said: that I
should never get drunk, that I should keep a clear
head, particularly if I was playing cards? Oh God!
Mama! Oh God! I had forgotten. The fever took
her so quickly… Where is the bottle?

8th March 1791

I was roused from my stupor this morning by the sound of my door opening and then footsteps which stopped by my bed, and then the curtains were pulled back and sunlight flooded the room. I groaned and clutched my head and said, 'Close the damn curtains. What is the matter with you?'

'It is twelve o'clock, time you were up,' said a voice I recognised.

'Darcy,' I said with a groan.

'This has gone on long enough. I cannot stand by and watch you sink any further.'

I put my head under the pillow.

'Just look at yourself,' he said, ripping the pillow from me and throwing a jug of water over me.

'Well?' I asked.

'I know we have grown apart, George, but

you were never like this. You were always so
careful with your appearance.'

I looked down, bleary eyed, at my clothes and
saw that they were dirty and creased, for I had
slept in them for God knows how long.

'I told you de Quincy was trouble. Where is
your comb?'

'Somewhere,' I said, waving towards my desk.

I heard him rummaging through the papers
and empty bottles and half-eaten sandwiches.

'You're worth more than this, George,' he
said. 'For a few weeks there's no harm in it,
but it can all too easily become a habit. Just
look at your desk,' he said, throwing an empty
bottle into the bin. 'Everything a mess, papers
everywhere…'

He stopped and there was a deathly silence.

'I had no idea,' he said, and I knew he had
found my father's letter. 'George, I am so sorry,
I had not heard.'

'Nothing to be sorry about,' I said, with a

feeling of hollowness. 'We live, we die, and there's an end of it.'

I pulled a half-empty bottle out from under the bed and put it to my lips, but he took it from me and sent for his valet.

'Get him up,' he said to the man when he arrived. 'I want him ready in half an hour. I am taking him to Pemberley.'

15th March 1791

I wish I was back at Cambridge. I am glad I am at home. Lord, I do not know what I think or what I feel; I do not know where I am or what I am doing. Nothing is the same. The house without Mama is not a home. Papa is broken. Mr Darcy is thoughtful. Fitzwilliam is kind. God damn him! Why could he not have left me alone?

7th May 1791

I avoided Peter de Quincy when I first returned to Cambridge, but he keeps seeking me out and it is easier to go along with him than resist him. Besides, he knows all the best people and, when he is not frequenting low taverns, he is introducing me to useful friends. I see less of Darcy than I used. Something about him makes me uncomfortable. He wants to save me, to put my feet on the right path, but his idea of the right path for me does not involve heiresses. On the few occasions I have seen him, I have rebuffed him.

21st May 1791

I went to a party, a respectable one, tonight and saw Darcy for the first time in weeks. He was looking very handsome. For a moment I was jealous, for I knew that my own body had started to show the signs of too much drinking and wenching and not enough signs of riding and fencing. I shrugged it off, but when I saw the women hanging on his every word and ignoring me, I knew I must do something about it. To be sure, a lot of it is to do with the fact that he is Darcy of Pemberley, but not all. And I must not forget that I intend to be Wickham of Rosings. It would not do to go to seed before I have my future secure.

23rd May 1791

I went to bed sober last night and got up early this morning. I had forgotten how much I enjoy being out of doors when the sun is rising. I felt invigorated and full of new energies. It is time to put the past behind me and look to the future.

27th May 1791

I went round to Darcy's rooms early this morning, and after a little coldness I confessed that he had been right and I had been wrong and that I had fallen into bad company. He looked relieved and offered me a horse to ride and we went out together, talking of Pemberley and our experiences at Cambridge and our futures.

'My father intends to give you the living at Pemberley,' he said, as we returned to our rooms, 'but I am not sure that you are suited to the church. Are you comfortable with the idea of preaching sermons, George? Because the church is not a profession to enter lightly. A clergyman has the good of his parishioners in his care and if he cannot set them an example…'

'My dear Darcy, I have learned my lesson,' I said, and I used all my charm to help me. 'It went to my head, the new place, the new people, the easy friendship, the parties, the... yes, why not say it?... the wine and the women. And then Mama... But such a life palls before long, and I do not think a man is any less fitted for the church because he has found this out through experience, rather than finding it out through the experience of others.'

'There is something in what you say.'

'To understand sinners, I have to understand their sins. I have to understand their temptations, too, for how else could I treat them with under-standing and grant them forgiveness?'

He was satisfied. Indeed, as I spoke, I more than half believed it myself. But I must be care-ful if I am not to lose his family's patronage. Mama was right: there is something implacable in Darcy, some strength of character that will not allow him to be bullied or persuaded out of doing what he thinks is right. Moreover, his good opinion, once lost, is never regained, a fact James learned to his cost, for when he approached

Fitzwilliam to help him with some trifling debts, Fitzwilliam refused him; he has never forgiven him for tormenting Georgiana by taking her doll, all those years ago.

I am lucky I did not lose his good opinion entirely this year and that he remained my friend. But I must be careful if I am to keep it, for until I marry an heiress, I need influential friends on my side.

30th October 1791

I have taken to carousing in London rather than Cambridge, where I comport myself with more or less dignity. Peter's family have a house there and we often escape and go to town, where we have several sweet little dancers and opera singers who keep us amused, as well as several taverns where the serving wenches are willing, when we are in a mood for lower company.

We were escorting two dancers back to our rooms tonight and were just having fun in the carriage when it stopped outside Peter's house at an inopportune moment.

'Oo, don't stop,' begged my partner, and like a gentleman I obliged, only to hear the door open.

I looked up, annoyed, only to see Darcy standing on the pavement!

By some ghastly chance he had been to the theatre and had decided to take a hackney cab home instead of walking. Thinking the station-ary cab was empty, he had opened the door, meaning to climb inside. He had then been con-fronted by more than he had seen since we were boys swimming naked together in the river at Pemberley, and more of Molly than anyone has ever seen without paying her.

To his credit, he simply raised his eyebrows, said, 'I beg your pardon, I did not know the cab was taken,' and closed the door again.

I burst out laughing, Molly did the same, and I hastily fastened my breeches and tumbled out of the cab.

'Darcy!' I called. 'Darcy! Wait.'

But he did not stop.

My little dancer followed me, for she had not been paid. I handed her what I owed her as I watched Darcy's retreating back and I thought, It is all up with me now.

I felt a sense of relief, for going into the church is not something I have any desire to do, no, not even for a large rectory and an easy living for the rest of my life. But I felt a sense of disappointment, too, that he should have found me like that.

Damn! Why is it that he makes me feel like that? Without ever saying a word he makes me feel inadequate.

But as he dwindled into the distance I felt a sense of sympathy too, for as I watched his retreating back it came over me that he was a lonely man, for all his money, his family, and his friends.

I remembered him telling me that he was looking for something.

Whatever it is, he has not found it.

I wonder if he ever will?

1794

7th June 1794

There are great changes at Pemberley. Old Mr Darcy has died. My father wrote to me and gave me the news.

> *I am sure you will be as sad as I am, George, for he was always a good friend to you, sending you first to Eton and then to Cambridge. And he has helped you even after his death, for he has left you a legacy of one thousand pounds and given instructions for Fitzwilliam to help you in your chosen profession. Are you still of a mind to go into the church? If so, you are to be given a valuable living.*

I put the letter down.

'Bad news?' asked Peter.

'Old Mr Darcy has died,' I said.

'What, Darcy of Pemberley?' asked Matthew, a new member of our set.

Matthew is a very good fellow, but alas! he is as poor as I am.

'Yes.'

'Then Fitzwilliam is now the master.'

'Yes,' I said.

'You are very thoughtful. Why?'

'Because it changes things.'

'How?'

'I am not sure. And that is why I am thoughtful. I think I must go home, Peter. Yes, in fact, I know I must. My future is changing.'

'Do you want it to? You have a sweet life here, George. Friends to amuse you, a good set of rooms, and a willing widow, with plenty of money to spend on you.'

'That is all very well,' I said thinking, 'but it will not do forever.'

'You surely do not mean to get rid of her? She has been very useful to you.'

'She has, but I have no mind to marry a widow, no matter how wealthy she is, especially one whose money came from a husband in such a low line of work. The widow of a gentleman, now, that might tempt me, if her position were high enough and she were rich enough. But no, not even then. I am too young to settle for a widow.'

'You are too young to settle at all,' he said.

'Yes, very true,' I said, pursing my lips. 'I have no desire to hurry into matrimony. But I must not neglect my future interests.'

He gave a shrug.

'Well, go if you must, but hurry back. You amuse me, George. Things won't be the same without you.'

9th June 1794

I found my father stricken with grief over the death of old Mr Darcy, for he was devoted to the old man.

'He gave me my chance in life, George. I had nothing before I came here; I was a simple country accountant. But by his good offices I had this house and a good income, and I know that both of them pleased your mother. And now he is gone.'

He sat silently for some minutes but then he roused himself and said, 'So, Fitzwilliam is the new master of Pemberley. He comes back here often, to spend time at home, but I seldom see you. Why is that, George?'

I felt uncomfortable, for the truth of the matter is that, without Mama, I have no desire to be at home; quite the reverse, I would rather be away. I could not tell him that, however, so

I said, 'I have to study, Father, you know that. Fitzwilliam does not need to work hard, but I do. He does not need to get his qualifications, he has no need of a career, but I must have a means of earning my own living. His time is his own, mine is not.'

He gave a sigh.

'True, true. I am glad to know that you are taking your future seriously. Your mother would have been proud of you. Have you had any more thoughts about your career? Do you still mean to go into the church?'

'I have not decided yet. Perhaps, or perhaps I might go into the law.'

'Well, they are both honourable professions. Fitzwilliam will help you whatever you decide to do, I am sure, for his father expressly asked him to do so in his will. They are all very affected at the big house. This death has come as a sad blow.'

I put on a grave face and said it was a sad blow to all of us.

My father then attending to his duties, I went out of the house and walked round the park, coming at last to the stables. I found Georgiana there and I remembered my mother saying that she would not be a little girl forever.

All the opportunities of home, which had been obscured by the pleasures of London, arose before me anew. I preferred Anne de Bourgh as a wife, for she was the richer of the two girls. However, I knew it would be sensible of me not to neglect Georgiana. And so I spoke to her kindly and invited her to ride with me and she did so, with a groom behind her. We spoke of her father and I said that he was a great man, and we spoke of Fitzwilliam and I said how proud I was to call him my friend, and I was pleased to discover that she did not know about the falling out between us.

We returned to the stables at last and I thought, as I had not thought for a long time: George Wickham of Rosings. Or George Wickham, husband to Georgiana Darcy.

20th June 1794

Old Mr Darcy is buried, and I am back in London, and now Fitzwilliam is the catch of the Season. Not that he will be going into society so soon after his father's death, but the drawing-rooms are already ringing with the sound of his name and of his income.

Peter and I laughed about it, but my laughter was tinged with envy, for Fitzwilliam can have his pick of heiresses without making any effort, whilst I have had little luck in securing one for myself. I have made enough friends at Cambridge to be sure of my share of invitations to the best balls, for a single man is always welcome at these things, especially if he dances, but I have not been able to catch an heiress. The girls are willing enough, but as soon as their mamas enquire into my fortune, they keep their daughters well away from me, whereas not one mama in London would keep her daughter away from Fitzwilliam Darcy.

17th November 1794

It is a year for deaths. Papa has followed old Mr Darcy to the grave.

And so now I am clearing out all my possessions, for the house is to be the new steward's house and I am to live here no more. I hinted to Darcy that I would like the position of steward, but he told me that the appointment had already been made and I knew better than to press him. His manner has been distant since the incident with the hackney cab and I am afraid that I have lost his good opinion. However, by means of a friendly and respectful demeanour every time I see him, I hope that, gradually, I might be able to wear down his resistance and make him, if not my friend, at least useful to me.

1795

5th April 1795

Peter's family have finally grown tired of his dissipated way of living and they have sent him out to the Indies, where one of his uncles is trying to make something of him. Not only have I lost his company, but my creditors are becoming a nuisance. Peter's friendship kept them complacent, but now that I do not have his backing they are sending in their accounts. I cannot believe I have spent so much money, for the bills come to almost two thousand pounds. Matthew and I were bemoaning the sad state of affairs, for he has run up debts that are almost as large as mine, when he said, 'I wonder you don't ask Darcy. Weren't the two of you friends?'

'We were but I will not ask him for money again. I did it once before and he gave me such a look that I have not asked again.'

'I don't see why he should refuse you. He has plenty of the stuff. A thousand pounds, to a man like Darcy, is nothing.'

It awakened all my resentful feelings.

'Darcy has always been that way. Even as a boy he treated me like a servant, not like an equal. He thought I would grow up to manage his estate. Can you imagine it? Me, to spend my life worrying about which trees to cut down and which trees to plant and which fields to put out to pasture? To think about incomings and outgoings?'

Matthew roared with laughter.

'If it was anything like the incomings and outgoings of your own pocket, the estate would be ruined in half a year! But won't he give you something? Surely, George, you must have some pressure you can bring to bear?'

'His father did promise me a living,' I said thoughtfully.

Matthew laughed even louder than before.

'What! He wanted you to be a clergyman? A fine job you would make of that!'

'I know,' I said, laughing too. 'It would never do. But it is a pity. The living would have meant a lot to me, or rather to my pockets.'

'Then ask him to give you the money instead.'

I looked at him in surprise.

'I didn't know you had a brain, Matthew.'

'Needs must, old fellow,' he said, taking a drink and savouring it. 'Needs must.'

'He would not give me anything just for the asking, that much I know, but perhaps there is a way.'

I thought about it, and then I went over to my desk and, dipping my quill in the ink and pulling a piece of paper towards me, I began to write.

After some preamble, hoping that both he and Georgiana were well and that the estate was prospering, I continued:

I have been giving some thought to my future and I have decided not to go into the church, and so I have decided to relinquish all claims to the living your father so generously promised me. I hope you will now be able to bestow it elsewhere.

I hope you will not think it unreasonable of me to ask for some kind of pecuniary advantage, instead of the living. I mean to go into the law, and as you are aware, the interest on one thousand pounds—the sum your father generously left me—does not go very far.

I went on to speak of generalities and then ended the letter, sanding it and folding it and sending it out at once to the mail.

'And now, let us go out and celebrate,' said Matthew. 'I have had some luck on the horses, and I mean to spend the evening in style.'

That is the good thing about Matthew. He might not be in the funds very often, but when he is, he is willing to share what he has.

We went first to an inn and then to a brothel, where we enjoyed ourselves immensely, and did not stumble home again 'til first light.

12th April 1795

At last, a letter from Darcy. It was stiff and formal in tone, with no hint of the friendship we once shared. However, he has offered me the sum of three thousand pounds to relinquish all claims to the living, both now and in the future, and I have accepted his terms. With three thousand pounds I can pay all my creditors and have some fun into the bargain.

Matthew called round and I told him it was my turn to treat him. We went to Vauxhall Gardens on the strength of my future riches, where we drank rack punch and followed the garishly dressed women into the dimly lit walks. There was plenty of fun to be had with them and we took full advantage of it.

At last we tired of them and returned to the more brightly lit areas. As we returned to our booth, a woman close by caught my eye. She was evidently a courtesan, well dressed and extremely beautiful, with thick dark hair and almond-shaped eyes. She felt me looking at her and turned towards me. She smiled, and I smiled back. She made some excuse to the man she was with and slipped out of her booth. I turned into one of the secluded corners of the Gardens and she followed me.

'Well?' I said.

'Well?' she said.

And then I kissed her and she kissed me back fervently, and we were soon lost to the world. At last, our hunger satisfied, we began to dress ourselves. She began to talk. She was witty and lively, mimicking her protector and saying she was tired of him. He was old and fat and she had a mind for someone younger. I told her, regretfully, that she was above my touch, even with my newfound funds, and she said that she was rich enough to settle for no more than a set of rooms for a while if I had a mind to take them for her.

We settled the thing then and there. She went back to the booth, where she told her lover their affair was at an end, and then went home with me, where we proceeded to enjoy ourselves some more, and then to learn something about each other.

'Belle,' I said musingly, when we lay back on the bed together. 'A beautiful name for a beautiful woman.'

'It is,' she said, then she began to laugh.

'What's the matter?' I asked.

'My real name's Gerty!' she said. 'Gerty Bertwhistle!'

We rolled on the bed, laughing, and could not stop. At last I wiped the tears from my eyes and said, 'Welcome, Gerty, to my humble abode. May you always make me laugh as much as you have tonight.'

'And may you always be as young and handsome as you are tonight,' she said.

'I'll drink to that.'

She joined me in the toast and we did not fall asleep until the bottle was empty.

1796

15th August 1796

Alas, Gerty and I have had to part. It has been coming for some time, for my pockets have become increasingly empty, and she has stayed with me for much longer than I could have expected, but now at last we have had to go our separate ways.

'You will soon find another protector,' I said.

'Yes, I think I will,' she said, studying herself critically in the mirror. 'But this will be the last one. My looks are going, and it's no life for a woman when she gets old.'

'What will you do afterwards?' I asked her.

'Who knows? Find a merchant to marry, maybe, or set up in business, perhaps. I might open a hat shop or a dress shop. You look after yourself, Georgie.'

'And you.'

She blew me a kiss and left without more ado.

I regretted her going. I have grown used to her. But there are plenty more women in the world, and all I have to do is to walk out of the door to find them.

More difficult is the question of how I am going to live. The money I had from Darcy is gone, and my credit is so long that, sooner or later, my creditors are going to start pressing me. I will have to live by my wits, for I have nothing else left to me, save my charm and my handsome face. And so between the three of them, they must earn me my keep and something more besides. They must earn me my future.

1798

18th August 1798

Once again I awoke to find a line of creditors at my door. I packed my bags hastily and slipped down the back stairs, only to find them waiting for me there as well.

And so I find myself in debtor's prison. I am only surprised I managed to avoid it for so long. My pockets are to let, my bills unpaid, and I have nowhere to turn.

23rd August 1798

At last! A piece of luck. I heard by chance that the living I should have had is vacant, the incumbent having recently died. I decided I would write to Darcy and remind him of the fact. I told him that I had decided against the law and decided instead to follow my original plan of being ordained and going into the church. I told him, too, that my circumstances were exceedingly bad and reminded him that his father intended me to have the Pemberley living. Then I posted the letter.

I only hope he helps me soon, for I am tired of kicking my heels in here and want to be out in life once again.

27th August 1798

I have had a reply from Darcy, and what a reply! To think that the boy I once went swimming with and fishing with could speak to me in such terms! He, who is no better than me, save for the fact that he was born into the Darcy cradle and not the cradle marked Wickham. How dare he? How dare he write me such a letter? How dare he refuse me the living and, what is more, say I am not fit to have it? How dare he refuse to help me, when it will cost him nothing? And how can he sit there in Pemberley, with not a care in the world, and leave me to the mercy of my creditors?

I was so angry I wrote and told him that his father would be ashamed of him and sent the letter straightaway. Once my anger had cooled I regretted it, for it would do no good and would only rouse his resentment, but it was done and could not be undone.

1799

21st January 1799

I mastered my anger and wrote again to Darcy, asking him to reconsider and reminding him again that it was his father's wish I should be provided for—reminding him, too, of the happy times we shared as boys. I only hope I said enough to make him change his mind.

23rd January 1799

Another refusal from Darcy. Damn him!

27th January 1799

I have written now three times to Darcy and each time he sends the same reply: that I must not expect anything further from him, that he has helped me all he intends to help me, and that I must now face up to the consequences of my actions and mend my ways before it is too late.

To hear him preaching to me made my blood boil. I was about to write to him again, angrily, for what did I have to lose, when something happened which distracted me. There was, visiting the prison, a woman who had come to bail out her sister. She cast an approving eye over me and I smiled in return. She spoke to me, I bowed to her, and the upshot is that she paid my bills and I am now living with her in her house.

'Why should I not have a pretty face to look at?' she asked, as she introduced me comfortably to her friends. 'I was a good wife to my dear

David, God bless him, and now that he's gone I want a bit of fun.'

It is a strange turn of events, and not one I wish to last, but for now, she is undemanding, generous, and appreciative, and it will do.

5th February 1799

I have grown tired of living off Mrs Dawson and her friends and I must think of another way to live. If one last appeal to Darcy does no good then I must find an heiress. And, fortunately, I know where one is to be found, for Anne de Bourgh is in Kent, and so to Kent I am bound.

27th February 1799

I arrived at the inn shortly after midday and took a room, then set about making discreet enquiries. I hoped to learn at what time Anne went out for her rides, so that I could happen to meet her and renew our friendship, but instead I learnt that the family were not at home.

I quickly conquered my disappointment and decided to look over the estate. I wanted to cheer myself by imagining my future as its lord and master. All problems of courting her under her mother's nose I chose, for the moment, to put aside.

I therefore set out, on horseback, and I was soon at the entrance to the park. It was magnificent. As I rode up the drive I could easily see myself as master of such an abode. The grounds would be ideal for house parties, for there would be plenty to do. Boating on the lake, fishing in the river, playing cricket on the lawn… and there was ample scope for children, too, with large trees to climb and all manner of outbuildings to hide in.

Indeed, by the time I had arrived at the door I already felt myself so much master of the house that I had no hesitation in going inside, where the housekeeper welcomed me warmly and said that she would be glad to show me round, for the family were in Bath on account of Miss Anne's health.

'It is a very fine house, Sir, the finest in Kent.'

'Is that so?'

'Oh, yes, Sir, the very finest, everyone knows it for such hereabouts. The de Bourghs have lived here for five hundred years, the name passing down through sons and daughters, for there is no entailment on the estate and so no difficulty about a female inheriting. The only stipulation is that the husband of any heiress of Rosings should take the family name.'

'Indeed?' I said, whilst thinking expansively, *I shall be George de Bourgh.*

'Oh, yes, indeed, sir, the family do not want the name to die out, you see.'

She stopped in front of the portraits hanging in the hall.

'That picture is of the present owner, Lady Catherine de Bourgh. The picture was to commemorate her wedding day.'

I looked at the picture of Lady Catherine, looking young and noble, and beside her Sir Lewis, a handsome young man with blue eyes and an amiable expression.

'And next to them is a portrait of their daughter, Miss Anne.'

I looked at the portrait and I was reminded of Anne as she was before her father's death, for although her pose was formal, there was laughter round her mouth and in her eyes.

If I could bring that Anne back I would have an amusing as well as a wealthy wife, and why should I not? As Mama was always so fond of saying, I could charm the birds from the trees.

We went into the drawing-room, and I admired its dimensions, which were truly impressive, and looked out onto the park. The view was discussed, and then we went over the rest of the house, or at least, all that was on display to visitors.

'Well, sir, what do you think of it, is it not the finest house you have seen?'

'It is excellent,' I said. 'I should not mind living here myself.'

She laughed, and I thought, We will laugh together when I return here as the master. It is a story she will tell to my children and grand-children. *When your father first came here, I showed him around the house and he said he should not mind living here himself. His words proved to be prophetic, for he married Miss Anne and now he is living here.*

When I had seen all there was to be seen I left the house, well pleased with my visit. I was so eager to have the place for my own that I decided not to wait for Anne to return; I decided to follow her to Bath.

1st March 1799

I have put my time in Bath to good use and I have discovered that Lady Catherine is staying in Laura Place. Miss Anne takes the waters at ten o'clock each morning and I mean to see here there tomorrow.

2nd March 1799

I was at the Pump Room by a quarter to ten and I contented myself with strolling round until I saw Anne enter the room out of the corner of my eye. To my delight she was not with her mother but was instead with her companion. I walked over to the Pump, timing myself so that I arrived there with Anne.

'Why, if it isn't Miss Anne!' I said in feigned surprise.

'Mr Wickham,' she said, with real surprise.

'What a strange chance meeting you here. What brings you to Bath?'

'I am here to drink the waters. My health is not good, alas.'

'I am here for the same purpose. I have had one or two trifling ailments recently and my physician felt it would set me up to come to Bath for a few weeks.'

We both took our glasses of the water and I was forced to drink the noxious stuff. I tried not to grimace, and Anne did the same, and we laughed together.

'It is horrible, is it not?' I said.

'It is,' she agreed.

'Look, over there, there is a chair, Miss Anne,' said her companion, trying to get her away from me.

But I was not to be so easily shaken.

'Let me escort you,' I said.

I gave her my arm and led her to the chair. Her companion glowered at me but I ignored her sour looks and said, 'I was very sorry to hear about Mr Darcy—old Mr Darcy, that is. It was a sad loss when he passed away.'

'Oh yes, it was,' she said.

'He was always a great friend to me,' I said respectfully. 'I believe he loved me almost as another son, and in return I loved him almost as another father. He had high hopes for me, and it has been the purpose of my life to make sure that I realise his dreams. He gave me the benefit of a gentleman's education and a gentleman's life at Pemberley, and I will always be thankful to him for his generosity in both deed and spirit.'

She smiled and said he had always been very kind to her, and the companion looked somewhat mollified at the idea that I was a gentleman and an intimate at Pemberley.

We were just beginning to get along very well when Lady Catherine arrived, throwing a gloom over the whole party. Anne's expression, which had started to become more animated, closed entirely, and the companion seemed ill at ease.

Lady Catherine looked at me pointedly.

'Your face is familiar,' she said.

'George Wickham,' I said, bowing. 'I had the pleasure of meeting you at Pemberley.'

'Ah, yes, I remember now,' she said, and I felt myself begin to relax. But then she said dismissively, 'The steward's son.' Then, turning away from me she said, 'Come, Anne, finish your drink; we are due at Lady Eleanor's in half an hour.'

Anne finished the noxious liquid and then, without so much as a glance at me, followed her mother from the room.

I do not intend to be so easily dismissed, however. I am sure that Anne is willing to know me, even if her mother is not. I discovered from other visitors that Miss de Bourgh frequents the library on a Thursday afternoon, and so, on Thursday, to the library I shall go.

5th March 1799

I was at the library in good time and, once again, I feigned surprise on seeing Anne. But this time there was no complaisance on the part of her companion.

'Mr Wickham, we will bid you good day,' she said. 'Miss de Bourgh, you know your Mama said we were not to be above ten minutes. We must change your books and then be on our way.'

I tried to start a conversation but it was no good. Anne was anxious, her companion watchful, and I had to withdraw with good grace.

I will bide my time, however. In a few years time Lady Catherine might have passed away, and then I can renew my assault.

3rd July 1799

Whilst walking through the park today, who should I see but Belle! She was as delighted to see me as I was to see her and we went to an inn together. The day was so hot that we both ordered an ice.

'And have you married your merchant?' I asked her, as we began to eat. 'You were going to find some rich husband and settle down the last time we met.'

'No, I changed my mind. I couldn't find anyone to suit me and in the end I decided that, anyway, it would not do. I am not cut out to be a wife. I have taken a salaried position instead.'

'Ah, so you are some man's mistress then. He is very lucky. I only wish I had more money, my dear, and I would snap you up myself.'

She laughed at me.

'Pockets to let as usual, George?'

'You know me too well,' I said, turning them out so that she could see how empty they were.

She raised her eyebrows and went back to her ice, but after a minute or two she said seriously, 'We're both getting older, George, even you are not as young as you were. You ought to be thinking of settling down. Marriage is easier for a man, not as restraining. With your silver tongue you ought to be looking for an heiress to marry.'

'I have been thinking in just the same way.'

She turned and looked at me appraisingly.

'What is it?' I asked.

'Only this. That I am engaged to be a companion—'

'A companion! I had no idea your salaried position would be so respectable,' I said. 'You will never keep it, Belle. You will not be able to hold your tongue when some old harridan starts telling you what to do.'

'I'm not engaged to be a companion to an old harridan, but to a young girl—'

'A young girl!' I exclaimed. 'You, Belle! Why, who would employ a woman like you to be a companion to a young girl—begging your pardon, but you know what I mean.'

'Don't worry, George, I know exactly what you mean. But you see my employer doesn't know about my history, and who is going to tell him? You?'

'No, of course not, but how did you come by such a post in the first place?' I asked curiously, for I could not imagine any way in which it could happen.

She took another spoonful of ice and let it melt slowly on her tongue, then said, 'I met an old school friend by chance in the circulating library. I went to an elegant seminary, you know, one of the best, a very respectable establishment it was, and frequented by some very good families. My family were respectable, God bless them, when they were alive. But when my parents died, shortly after I left the seminary, I had to fend for myself and—well, you know the rest. Well, I met this friend again, Amelia Campbell, and we exclaimed over the chance and then caught up on all the news, only my version of my history was, as you may well guess, a slightly altered one.'

'Did she not suspect anything? Had she not heard anything of you in the meantime?'

'No, not she. She had married a man in the diplomatic corps and so had spent many years abroad, and she and her husband had only just returned to this country. So she had heard nothing of my years in the *demimonde*. She saw what she expected to see: an old school friend, somewhat shabbily dressed but as respectable as ever. I quickly saw she could be of use to me, and so I spun her a tale about how I had married a wonderful man, how happy we had been until his tragic death in a carriage accident, my brave struggle to manage since his death, and my poor but respectable life. She, bless her, was full of sympathy and said she knew of an excellent position that might suit me, and before the week was out I was employed. So tomorrow I am to take up my new appointment and in a few weeks we are to go to Ramsgate, where my young lady is to spend the summer; her brother thinks it is too hot for her in London and he wants her to have the benefit of sea air.'

'And you have a plan in mind?' I asked her.

'Yes, I have, George. This young woman is an heiress.'

I saw where her thoughts were tending and I began to take more interest in her story.

'An heiress, under your influence,' I said thoughtfully. 'And she is to spend the summer at a seaside resort, where she will not be watched very closely. She will be away from her family?'

'She will. She will be there alone with me. She is an orphan,' she said by way of explanation.

'Better and better. If she is all alone in the world—'

'No, not that. She has a brother, a careful guardian, but he will not be going with her to the seaside. He will, for the most part, remain in London. He has property in the country as well, and he spends his time between the two places, managing his affairs.'

'Then whilst he is busy we will snatch his gem, if she is worth it. How large is her fortune?' I asked.

Belle gave a wide smile.

'Thirty thousand pounds.'

I sat up at that.

'Thirty thousand pounds?' I asked, my head already whirling.

'Aye, thirty thousand pounds. That's made you sit up straight. She's a prize worth winning, eh?'

'She is indeed,' I said.

Thirty thousand pounds! What could I not do with such a sum! I need never be poor again.

'I would want my share,' said Belle.

'Of course. You can have a thousand pounds—'

'Now, George, don't be mean, I would rather have two.'

'I will be the one running all the risks,' I reminded her.

'What risks?' she said in derision. 'There aren't any risks.'

I pushed the ice away from me and leant forward.

'Yes there are,' I said. 'If her brother finds out what I'm doing and calls me out, then it will be me looking down the wrong end of a pistol, not you, and if he is a good shot then it will be me taking the bullet.'

'He will have to catch you first.' She laughed and finished off her ice with one last lick of the spoon. 'And how will he find out? By the time he learns that anything is amiss you will be half-way to Scotland.'

'Scotland?' The word brought me up short. 'She is under age then?'

'Yes. She is fifteen.'

'That is very young,' I said with a frown.

'In England, yes, though in Scotland it is thought plenty old enough to be married and no parents' or guardian's consent needed, just two people who say they want to be wed. Then it's a quick ceremony over the anvil and you're legally man and wife—or perhaps I should say man and fortune!' she added, laughing.

I joined in her laughter.

'Man and fortune. I like that,' I said. Then I became serious. 'Now, how is the thing to be done?'

She thought.

'You must meet us casually,' she said at last. 'A chance meeting, in the circulating library…'

'No, not the library; there will be too many people there and too many curious glances. We should meet somewhere less crowded, whilst walking by the sea perhaps, somewhere well away from the main promenade, so that there will be very few people there. Then I can scrape an acquaintance—perhaps we have friends in common, or anyway I can at least pretend we have. What is her name?'

'Darcy,' she said.

I stared at her.

'Darcy?' I asked in astonishment.

'Yes. Why, do you know her?' she asked.

'Not *Georgiana* Darcy?' I said.

'Yes. Why?' she asked curiously. 'Do you know her?'

I began to smile and then I fell back laughing. I could not believe it! It was too good a joke.

'Know her? Yes, I know her! I practically grew up with her! I lived on the same estate and I was an intimate of her family. I was her brother's friend and her father's favourite. But this is capital. Georgiana Darcy! It will be child's play to win her confidence and then elope with her.'

'If you're a friend of her brother, then why…?'

'I *was* a friend of her brother,' I said. 'But that was a long time ago. I am no longer a friend of

Darcy's; he's treated me too badly for us to ever be friends again. But that's what makes it so delicious. I can not only win myself an heiress for a wife when I run away with Georgiana, I can also be revenged on him at the same time.'

'You seem to hate him. Has he injured you so badly?' she asked, looking at me closely.

'Oh. Yes, he has injured me very badly, and in very many ways,' I said, my mood darkening. 'As a boy he treated me as a servant, someone who would spend my life waiting on him, and then when we were grown he was always trying to tell me how to behave, until at the end he destroyed my life entirely by robbing me of my living.'

'Why? How did he do that?' she asked, agog.

'By refusing to honour the express wishes of his father. The old man had liked me very much and he had provided for my by giving me a good education and then leaving me a living in his will...'

'You don't mean a *religious* living?' she asked in astonishment.

'Yes, I do,' I said. 'It was a very valuable one at that, with a gentleman's residence attached to it, a very fine rectory in large grounds, and a good income. But Darcy refused to honour his father's wishes. Can you believe it, Belle, the self-righteous prig told me I wasn't fit to hold the living and that therefore I must do without it?'

She burst out laughing.

'Oh, George, I'm sorry, but really it is too ridiculous! You! A clergyman! Standing up in church, giving sermons, and telling other people how to live their lives!'

'I would have made a very good clergyman,' I said, annoyed. 'I can give a sermon as well as anyone else, yes, and tell them what to do, too. I can do everything else the clergy do as well. I can eat too much and drink too much and collect my tithes… but the living was denied me,' I ended bitterly.

'Ah yes, I remember now, I seem to think I heard you talking about it. But I thought you said you gave it up in return for some money?'

'I gave it up *temporarily*,' I said, 'being in low funds and needing something on account with which to pay my bills. But when it became vacant—'

'—And you found you needed some money again—'

'—I said that I was ready to take it. Darcy refused to give it to me, even though he knew my situation was desperate and even though I asked him for it several times. At last I gave up asking for it and we have not spoken since.'

'And now you are in a position to secure your future by running away with his sister,' she said slowly.

'With your help, yes, I am. I will have a good living, far better than the one he refused me, because I will not have to do anything for it: no reading or writing of sermons, no dressing soberly and pretending to care about everyone in my parish. Well, Belle, are you still going to help me?' I asked her, putting my bad humour aside and turning towards her with a winning smile.

'Of course I am,' she said. 'Never you mind, George, what's done is done, and you're right to look to the future instead of dwelling on the past. I'll help you catch your heiress, and gladly.' I squeezed her hand and she smiled at me. 'She's a lucky girl. I only wish I had a fortune and then I'd marry you myself. You're a handsome man, George, and you know how to make yourself attractive to a woman. It will be easy. I will help you by encouraging her romantic notions—'

'Let her read *Romeo and Juliet*.'

'A good idea. And I will talk to her about the romance of elopements: a carriage ride through the night, the moon up above, a rosy-cheeked blacksmith in Gretna Green, and a marriage over the anvil. Two people plighting their troth, making their vows to each other in a private ceremony that celebrates everything that is real and good without all the fuss of a society wedding, where half the people do not even know the bride and groom. I might even tell her that I eloped myself, and that I never regretted it, because the memories are amongst my most cherished.'

I smiled at her.

'It must be fate that brought you to me again,' I said. 'I don't mind telling you, Belle, I thought I was done for. I had no money and no chance of getting any. But now, the future looks rosy again.'

'I reckon fate brought you to me again, too. I was feeling restless and beginning to wish I'd never taken on the job as a companion; it was too staid for me. But you've injected some fun into it. You always were fun, George,' she said, leaning forward to display her ample bosom and then brushing my cheek with her hand. 'What do you say? Once more, for old times' sake?'

'You know I could never resist you,' I said, catching her hand and kissing it.

'I have a set of rooms just round the corner.'

She gave me the address and then she left. I waited a few minutes and then I followed her and we resumed our happy friendship.

4th July 1799

I went to the tailor's today to order a new coat and then stopped at the jewellers to buy a diamond pin for my cravat. I had to go to the less fashionable establishments where I was not known, otherwise the shopkeepers would never have given me credit, but what do I care about such small matters now? All that was in the past. Before long I will have credit everywhere again, not only as a wealthy man, courtesy of his wife's fortune, but also as a member of the Darcy family. What a wonderful thing fate is! Not only is it going to bring me a wealthy bride, it is going to make me Darcy's relation. In a few weeks time, he will no longer be able to regard me as a servant; he will have to call me his brother-in-law!

12th July 1799

I had a letter from Belle this morning. She and Georgiana are settled in Ramsgate. As they do not know anyone, there will be no danger of anyone seeing me paying my addresses and no one to interfere. Darcy has no plans to visit, being too busy with business at the moment, and so it is time for me to put my plan into action. I am looking forward to it. Revenge and riches! What more could a man want? The summer promises to be an interesting one.

15th July 1799

A fine day, exactly the sort of day I wanted, with a smiling sea, a gentle breeze, a blue sky and white clouds floating across it. The poets themselves could not have designed a better day for my purposes.

At eleven o'clock exactly I set out from my lodgings. At a quarter to twelve, I saw Belle walking along the promenade towards me with her charge. I was elated to see that Georgiana was even more beautiful than I expected. Her figure was light and pleasing, her complexion was clear, her eyes were dark and lovely and her hair was thick and lustrous.

I carried on walking and we drew level and then I feigned a look of surprise and said, 'Why, if it isn't Georgiana! Or Miss Darcy I should say.'

I turned the full force of my charm on her and she exclaimed, 'George!'

The delight in her voice went straight to my heart, or I should say, straight to my pocket.

Belle, playing her part magnificently, said to Georgiana, 'Do you know this gentleman, Miss Darcy?'

'Oh, forgive me, Mrs Younge. Of course you do not know him, but yes, I do. I should not have spoken to him if we were not acquainted, I do assure you. This is…'

'Mr George Wickham, at your service, ma'am,' I said, making Belle a low bow. 'An old friend of the Darcys.'

'Oh!' said Belle, her voice warming. 'You are known to Mr Darcy?'

'I am indeed.'

'George grew up with Fitzwilliam,' said Georgiana. Then she hesitated, as though remembering that recently we had not been friends.

Belle took her opportunity, however, and said, 'In that case, you must join us for dinner, Mr Wickham. If you are willing to take potluck we will be honoured to see you. Will we not, Miss Darcy?'

'Oh, yes,' said Georgiana, overcoming her brief anxiety. 'Yes, we will. It is nice to see a familiar face.'

'And a friendly face,' I said to her. Then, turning to Belle, I said, 'Thank you for the invitation. I would be delighted to accept.'

'Then we will see you at six o'clock,' she said.

I bowed and walked on, returning to my lodgings by a circuitous route.

It was not until a few hours later, at two o'clock, that I learned how Georgiana had reacted to our meeting; Belle, on pretence of ridding herself of a headache, had excused herself from her charge and once again taken a walk by the sea.

'Where is Georgiana?' I asked.

'Practising the pianoforte. Have no fear. She will not discover us. She is very obedient and will not venture out of the house without my permission.'

'You did well to seize the moment and invite me to dinner,' I said. 'I saw her wavering and I thought we were undone. Has she said anything to you about me?'

'Yes. She said that she was not sure her brother would like you joining us for dinner because the two of you had argued. I said that she should not trouble herself about it, that men were always arguing about politics or business or world affairs and that it meant nothing. She relented at that and said that the girls at her seminary were often arguing as well, but that the arguments were soon forgotten. Then I sealed the matter by asking her if her father had approved of you and she said that yes, you were a great favourite of his. So I told her that, in that case, she was right to offer you hospitality and extend to you every courtesy. You have only to flatter her a little and look at her appreciatively and the thing will soon be done.'

'Good. The sooner the better. We do not

want Darcy ruining our plans. He has no intention of coming here, I hope?'

'He intends to call at the end of the month but not before, so you need not worry about it. By then your work will be done and you will be in Scotland.'

'Ah! Scotland. It is a long time since I was there. I think I might stay there for a few weeks and give the fuss a chance to die down. Georgiana can write to Darcy once we are married, and then a tour of the highlands will give us a chance to lose ourselves until Darcy has had time to accustom himself to the idea and to accept it. And what do you intend to do, once Georgiana has gone?'

'I intend to be found searching for her, saying that I am beside myself with worry for she went to her room as usual the night before but when her maid went to draw back the curtains in the morning she had gone. I intend to hand him a note saying that she had eloped with the man of her dreams and then I intend to say that I have guarded her carefully and that she has not spoken to any young men, except his friend Mr Wickham.'

I laughed.

'I wish I could be there to see his face when he hears my name.'

'If you are there to see his face he will see yours and then you are ruined,' she said. 'You must be well away before that happens, safely in Scotland, indeed safely married. Where will you go after your tour? You cannot stay in the highlands forever.'

'To London, perhaps, or to the country, to buy a home of our own. A large house in ample grounds, a gentleman's residence, with a river running through it. We can entertain there. We can invite Darcy to dinner!'

'I wouldn't mind a little home in the country myself,' said Belle. 'Nothing so grand as what you have in mind, but a comfortable little place with a maid to wait on me. I might buy something in your neighbourhood.'

'Do, Belle, and we can carry on our friendship at close quarters. We will celebrate our luck together!' I envisioned a happy future, with Belle to entertain me and Georgiana to be my beautiful, and very wealthy, wife. 'But for now you had better go back or she will be missing you. I will see you at six o'clock.'

She hurried off and I returned to my lodgings, where a willing little chambermaid awaited me. I passed the afternoon pleasantly enough and then dressed with care, presenting myself punctually at Georgiana's house. It was a respectable dwelling, nothing too large, but ideally suited to being a young lady's summer residence. I was shown in, and there was Georgiana looking very beautiful, her Darcy profile classically handsome, her figure graceful and elegant. Her dress was very costly and her shoes, dyed to match, were as expensive as her dress. She rose to meet me and I caught the scent of lavender and roses.

Belle stood respectfully behind her, looking demure and respectable.

Georgiana was suddenly overcome with shyness, for she was not used to the role of hostess, and so Belle prompted her, saying, 'Miss Darcy.'

Georgiana looked flustered but she welcomed me all the same, saying, 'Mr Wickham, welcome,' with all the consciousness of a young lady welcoming a guest for the first time on her own.

'Thank you, Georgie—but I must not call you that, you are a young lady now and not a child. I must call you Miss Darcy,' I said with a charming smile.

She blushed but she looked pleased, and Belle cast me an approving glance.

'Won't you ask Mr Wickham to sit down?' said Belle.

'Oh, yes, please George, do sit down,' said Georgiana.

Belle and I exchanged glances, for neither of us had missed Georgiana's use of my name, and then I turned back to Georgiana.

She sat down and I followed suit, placing myself in a chair opposite her.

'What a coincidence, your names being so similar, George and Georgiana, just like they are a pair,' said Belle, filling the silence, for Georgiana was shy.

'When I was younger, my mother called me Georgie, and Georgiana was also called by that name,' I said, looking at Belle and then turning and smiling in a friendly fashion at Georgiana, who smiled in return.

'I think you said your mother lived in Ramsgate, Mr Wickham?' asked Belle, knowing I had said no such thing but wanting to give me an opportunity to speak.

'No, alas, my mother is dead,' I said.

And I felt real regret as I said it.

'As mine is,' said Georgiana.

We exchanged sympathetic glances.

'I can see you have much in common,' said Belle.

'Indeed,' I said. 'We both lost our fathers some years ago, my father following Miss Darcy's father to the grave within a matter of months. He was Mr Darcy's steward.'

'A fine occupation, and a very necessary one,' said Belle. 'Suitable for a gentleman, and yet at the same time of great use. So many gentlemen these days seem to fritter their time away on nothing. Miss Darcy and I were talking about it only the other day. Do you have a profession, Mr Wickham?'

'Yes, I intend to go into the law.'

'A noble calling,' said Belle approvingly. 'Do you not have family members in the law, Miss Darcy?' asked Belle. 'Was not your uncle a judge?' Georgiana said that yes, that was so, and Belle remarked comfortably that interests in common were so important to friendship and she was sure she was delighted that Miss

Darcy had found such a suitable companion in Ramsgate. 'For the people hereabouts are not all of the right kind. You must ask Mr Wickham if he would care to join us for a picnic on the downs tomorrow,' said Belle to Georgiana. 'I would have suggested it last week, but without a gentleman to lend me his arm I could not have managed the hill and even you, my dear, I am persuaded would have found it difficult. But with a gentleman those kinds of things are so much easier.'

Georgiana invited me on the picnic and I accepted, saying I would be delighted to offer the ladies any assistance they might require.

It was time for dinner, and as we ate, we planned several excursions for the coming weeks. Georgiana became animated as we discussed picnics and boating parties, and by the time dinner was over she had lost her shyness around me and was treating me as she had done in the days, long gone, when we were all children together. Cries of, 'Do you remember, George, when…?' or 'Did we not have fun on the day…?' led to shared memories, and Belle smiled at us both benignly as we talked over old times.

'And how is your playing coming along?' I asked Georgiana as we moved into the drawing-room after dinner. 'You always had a musical touch, though you were not always inclined to practise,' I teased her.

'Miss Darcy is a proficient,' said Belle. 'She excels at music; everybody says so. Her masters are very pleased with her. So are we all. Play something for Mr Wickham, my dear. That pretty tune you were practising this morning, perhaps.'

Georgiana sat down at the instrument and played a lively sonata. She really played well, and as I sat and watched her, I thought, I will make her happy. She will want for nothing as my wife. She will have clothes, jewels, a piano-forte, a horse, and a fine house to live in. And when Fitzwilliam sees how happy she is with me he will forgive me everything, particularly when the children come along, for then he will have nephews and nieces to strengthen the attachment between us. We will visit Pemberley at Christmas and Rosings at Easter and before very long, perhaps he will decide to do something for us and Georgiana and I will have an estate of our own.

As I thought of Darcy I remembered him as a lonely figure, surrounded by friends and yet somehow out of their reach. I remembered him saying that he was looking for something. I wondered if he had found it. I had certainly found what I was looking for, a rich, beautiful, and well-connected wife. So at ease did I feel, so at peace with the world, that I hoped he had found what he was looking for, too.

Georgiana finished her sonata and I congratulated her warmly. She smiled at my praise and Belle and I exchanged glances again. It would be easy to win her affections and make her agree to an elopement.

I have a few weeks in which to woo her and then it will be off to Gretna Green and a wedding over the anvil.

16th July 1799

The weather could not have been more perfect for our picnic. I hired a carriage for the first part of the journey, but when we reached the downs I helped the ladies out. Then, giving them each an arm, I escorted them to a beauty spot with the coach driver carrying the basket. I thanked him for his trouble, paid him handsomely, and then set about helping the ladies to all the choice delicacies contained in the hamper.

Afterwards, Belle declared herself too tired to walk any further but said that we must not let that stop us, for she would enjoy watching us as much as she would have enjoyed walking with us.

I gave Georgiana my arm and we set off.

Luck was on my side. We had not been walking for more than five minutes when a sudden gust of wind blew her bonnet off and sent it tumbling down the hill. We both ran after it, just like children again, and did not see our danger until it was almost too late, for the downs fell away suddenly and Georgiana nearly ran over the edge. I caught her hand and pulled her back, dragging her into my arms. Our faces were inches apart and I felt her body melt into mine and I knew that she was attracted to me. I let her go, and I saw the reluctance in her eyes as she was forced to step away from me.

'I am glad I found you again, Georgie,' I said.

'As am I,' she whispered, overcome with confusion.

'I am afraid your bonnet is lost,' I said, as I watched the wind carry it out to sea. 'But never fear, I will buy you another one.'

'Oh, there is no need, I know you cannot afford it!' she said.

I smiled.

'What, do you think I am a pauper?'

'Fitzwilliam says that your pockets are always to let,' she told me.

'When I was a student then yes, I admit, I spent unwisely, but I am older and wiser now. Young men are apt to be foolish, but maturity cures the problem you know.'

I gave her my arm and she hesitated.

'Come now, we are old friends, are we not?' I said.

She smiled shyly and took my arm. I covered her hand with my own and she looked up at me, her eyes drawn to mine. I looked steadily into her eyes and then, when her eyelids began to droop and her head inclined towards me of its own will, I said, 'We must go back.'

She blushed and said, 'Of course,' and we walked back to Belle.

Belle had seen everything and cast a triumphant glance at me.

We had had the best of the weather. Clouds started to cover the sky and the breeze became colder. We gathered our things together and we went back to the carriage, just as it began to rain, and we were soon on our way back down to the town. I took my leave of the ladies and went to the milliners, where I bought the most beautiful bonnet in the window. And then I went to an out-of-the-way inn and entertained myself with a willing wench until the early hours.

17th July 1799

I called on Georgiana this morning, taking the bonnet with me.

'I promised you a new one, you see, and I do not forget my promises,' I said.

She looked doubtful and said that she could not accept it, but Belle said, 'If Mr Wickham was a stranger you would be right to refuse, for a lady should never accept a gift from a gentleman. But as he is such a friend of the family there is no harm in it, my dear, particularly as it is not a gift at all, really; it is only to replace the bonnet you lost.'

Thus encouraged, Georgiana tried on the bonnet and smiled as she saw how becoming it was.

'You have grown into a beauty,' I told her, turning the full force of my charm on her. 'The man who wins you will be lucky indeed.'

She blushed and turned away, but I saw her

face in the mirror and she was looking happy and excited.

The boating outing this afternoon brought us even closer, for as she climbed into the sailing boat, she wobbled, and I had to catch hold of her and assist her bodily into the boat. I sat close to her throughout the voyage and twice she clutched at my arm when a large wave rocked the boat, and then again, when we disembarked, I had to render her my assistance.

Offering her my arm on the way back to her house, I felt her lean on me much more heavily than she had done previously, and press closer to me, and I thought that the time was soon approaching when I would be able to propose.

Belle invited me in but I declined her invitation, knowing that absence would make Georgiana's heart grow fonder. And it did, for her eyes followed me regretfully as I left the house.

In only a few more days, or a week, perhaps, I will ask her to marry me. There is no sense in delaying. As soon as I am certain of success I will proceed. The sooner we are in Scotland the better.

27th July 1799

I met Belle this morning, walking by the sea, whilst Georgiana was busy indoors with her watercolours. Belle's 'headaches' are proving to be very useful as they give us a chance to talk. We met far away from the main promenade, where we would not be observed.

'How does Georgiana seem this morning? Does she speak of me?'

'All the time. She is head over heels in love with you, and I am not surprised. That new coat looks very well on you. It would turn the head of a more experienced girl than Georgiana.'

'Is she ready yet for me to propose do you think?' I asked her.

'Yes, she is, I am sure of it. I encouraged her to take a number of romances out of the library when we first arrived here and yesterday, as she sat and read, I told her that her novel reminded me of my own happy life. I told her that I had met the most wonderful man in the world, kind, handsome, and a good friend, and that we had eloped together. She was shocked at first, but as I spoke about it she began to see how romantic it had been and in the end she was convinced that an elopement was the best way to marry, just a woman and her beloved plighting their troth together. After much sighing and smiling, I ended by wishing her the same happiness I had found.'

'That all sounds very promising. I will come round to dinner tonight and then I will propose tomorrow,' I said.

'Call on us at ten in the morning,' she said. 'I will take care to be out of the room when you arrive, and you can have five minutes alone. Is that long enough?'

'Yes. Five minutes is all I will need.'

28th July 1799

I dressed with great care this morning and I wore the cologne I know Georgiana likes. I called at the house at exactly ten o'clock, and, as Belle had promised, Georgiana was by herself. I was shown into the drawing-room and she started up, took a step towards me, then stopped and coloured, and said that Mrs Younge was upstairs.

'But she has only gone to fetch her workbasket. She will be down directly,' she said.

'I cannot say that I am sorry to have found you alone,' I said, going over to her and taking her hand, then kissing it impulsively before looking deeply into her eyes. 'Georgiana, you must know, you must have felt how much I like you. In our childhoods we were always friends, but, now that we are grown, my feelings for you have deepened, and I find that friendship is no longer enough for me. I love you, Georgiana, with all my heart and soul. I have no right to ask it, no right to expect it, but'—I sank to my knees in a very pretty gesture of submission—'will you do me the very great honour of becoming my wife?'

She blushed and smiled and said, 'It is you who do me too much honour, George.'

'Does that mean that you accept?' I asked, standing up and touching her cheek.

'Yes, it does. As long as Fitzwilliam gives his consent to the marriage, I will be your wife.'

'Then you have made me the happiest of men,' I said, kissing her hand again.

Belle, who had been listening at the door, then entered the room and said, 'Oh, Mr Wickham, how good of you to call.'

'I had something very particular I wanted to say to Miss Darcy,' I said.

'Oh?'

'Mr Wickham has asked me to be his wife,' said Georgiana.

Belle clapped her hands together in delight.

'Oh, this is wonderful news,' she said. 'The best news possible. I cannot say I am surprised. You two were made to be with each other. I knew it from the first moment I saw you together. Just like my good, dear Stephen and me. Oh, the happy times we had together, from the moment we met, to all the magic of our wedding in Scotland, to all the happy years we had together until he died. I only hope you two young people can have the same.'

'Why should we not?' I asked, as though suddenly struck by the idea. 'Why should we not go to Scotland?' I turned to Georgiana. 'What do you say to the idea, my love? Just you and me, pledging our love for each other, with none of the pomp and circumstance of more trivial marriages, marriages contracted for the sake of family connections or for the sake of convenience. Then there needs to be a show, for there is nothing else to unite the two people. But for us, who love each other dearly, there is no need for it. We need nothing but each other.'

Georgiana was carried away by the idea of it and we made our arrangements then and there, with Belle adding her comments every now and again to help the matter along.

'I left the house with only a bandbox,' said Belle. She was so convincing with her reminisces that even I almost believed her stories. 'My dear Stephen was waiting for me with a carriage at the end of the road.'

'Were your family not worried?' asked Georgiana, as she began to think of the matter more carefully.

'Bless you, no,' said Belle. 'I did not just run off, you know; I left a letter explaining everything. I would not have worried them for the world! My papa said afterwards that it was the most romantic letter he had ever read. He said that that was when he knew I was really in love, when he knew I would do without all the fripperies that went with a wedding, just to be with the man I loved.'

Georgiana looked at me and I smiled.

'If you want a large society wedding then we will have one. I would not deny you any pleasure for the world. But if you would like something more romantic then we will go to Scotland. The scenery there is very beautiful and the people are warm and friendly. Well, my love, what shall it be? Shall we elope?' She smiled and I took that as her answer. 'Very well, then, I will arrange the carriage for tomorrow, and then on to Scotland,' I said.

'Oh, yes, George.' Then she faltered. 'What about when we return? What will we do then?'

'We will buy a house and surprise all our friends by throwing a party to celebrate our marriage,' I said.

I left her then. I had no fear of her changing her mind, for I knew Belle would spend the rest of the day encouraging her in her plans for the future.

29th July 1799

A calamity! I am undone!

I hired the carriage and was just about to set off to collect Georgiana, with our route to Scotland firmly planned in my mind, when who should I see but Belle, hurrying down the road towards me.

I knew at once that something was wrong, and I called out for the coachman to stop.

'Fly!' she said, when she reached the carriage. 'Go! It is Mr Darcy! He has found us out! He called on us not an hour ago, wanting to surprise his sister, and she, poor fool, could not bear to deceive him and told him everything. He is in a towering rage. He is ready to murder you. You must be gone from here before he finds you, or who knows what he will do?'

I could not believe it. To be so near and yet so far.

'Damn!' I said. 'Damn Fitzwilliam Darcy! Was he born to ruin everything for me? First he denies me a living and now he denies me a wife.'

'Do not stay!' Belle begged me. 'Go, now, at once. He is a powerful man. He has friends, influence; he could make things very difficult for you.'

I looked at Belle with her comely face and figure and I thought, Why shouldn't I have some company on my flight.

'Come with me,' I said impulsively, seizing the moment.

'Come with you?' she asked in surprise.

'Yes, come with me, Belle. You cannot stay here. The carriage is waiting. We can go to Scotland together. Oh! Not to marry, but to have an adventure and get away from this dreary place. We will yet grab some pleasure from the day.'

She was undecided and then, suddenly picking up her skirt and climbing into the carriage beside me she said, 'Aye, what do I have to stay for?'

We were soon away, and before very long we had decided that we could be just as happy in London as in Scotland, and for a lot less expense, and so thither we went.

It was not what I expected from today, but what is the use of repining? Something will turn up, I am sure of it, and for now I have Belle to keep me company.

Besides, there is always still Anne de Bourgh.

4th November 1799

Our money has at last run out. Belle has invested what little she had left in a boarding house, and we have reluctantly decided to go our separate ways.

I am thinking of enlisting. One of my acquaintances happened to recommend his regiment to me this morning, and as I have nothing better to do I believe I will join. It will get me away from London, where my creditors are once again pressing me, and take me into Hertfordshire, a place where I am not known. Then I can begin again, and at the very least, run up some new bills.

And at the most… There will be impressionable young women in Meryton, no doubt, and they will all be susceptible to a charming and handsome young man in a red coat.

Who knows? I might meet my heiress in Hertfordshire, and by this time next year I might have eloped!

About the Author

Amanda Grange was born in Yorkshire, England, and spent her teenage years reading Jane Austen and Georgette Heyer whilst also finding time to study music at Nottingham University. She has had seventeen novels published, including five Jane Austen retellings which look at events from the heroes' points of view. *Woman* said of *Mr Darcy's Diary:* 'Lots of fun, this is the tale behind the alpha male,' whilst the *Washington Post* called *Mr Knightley's Diary* 'affectionate.' *The Historical Novels Review* made *Captain Wentworth's Diary* an Editors' Choice, remarking, 'Amanda Grange has taken on the challenge of reworking a much loved romance and succeeds brilliantly.'

Austenblog declared that *Colonel Brandon's Diary* was 'the best book yet in her series of heroes' diaries.' *Mr Darcy, Vampyre,* her paranormal sequel to *Pride and Prejudice,* was nominated for the Jane Austen Awards.

Amanda's stories have appeared in a number of collections including *Loves Me, Loves Me Not*; *The Mammoth Book of Regency Romance*; and *A Darcy Christmas.* Amanda Grange now lives in Cheshire, England. To learn more about her books, please visit her website at www.amandagrange.com.

Mr. Darcy's Diary

AMANDA GRANGE

"A gift to a new generation of Darcy fans
and a treat for existing fans as well." —**AUSTENBLOG**

The only place Darcy could share his innermost feelings…

…was in the private pages of his diary. Torn between his sense of duty to his family name and his growing passion for Elizabeth Bennet, all he can do is struggle not to fall in love. A skillful and graceful imagining of the hero's point of view in one of the most beloved and enduring love stories of all time.

What readers are saying:

"A delicious treat for all Austen addicts."

"Amanda Grange knows her subject…I ended up reading the entire book in one sitting."

"Brilliant, you could almost hear Darcy's voice…I was so sad when it came to an end. I loved the visions she gave us of their married life."

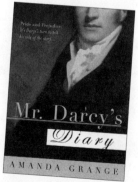

"Amanda Grange has perfectly captured all of Jane Austen's clever wit and social observations to make *Mr. Darcy's Diary* a must read for any fan."

978-1-4022-0876-8 • $14.95 US/ $19.95 CAN/ £7.99 UK

MR. DARCY, VAMPYRE

PRIDE AND PREJUDICE CONTINUES...

AMANDA GRANGE

"A seductively gothic tale…" —Romance Buy the Book

A test of love that will take them to hell and back…

My dearest Jane,

My hand is trembling as I write this letter. My nerves are in tatters and I am so altered that I believe you would not recognise me. The past two months have been a nightmarish whirl of strange and disturbing circumstances, and the future…

Jane, I am afraid.

It was all so different a few short months ago. When I awoke on my wedding morning, I thought myself the happiest woman alive…

"Amanda Grange has crafted a clever homage to the Gothic novels that Jane Austen so enjoyed." —*AustenBlog*

"Compelling, heartbreaking, and triumphant all at once."
—*Bloody Bad Books*

"The romance and mystery in this story melded together perfectly… a real page-turner." —*Night Owl Romance*

978-1-4022-3697-6
$14.99 US/$18.99 CAN/£7.99 UK

"Mr. Darcy makes an inordinately attractive vampire… *Mr. Darcy, Vampyre* delights lovers of Jane Austen that are looking for more."
—*Armchair Interviews*

WILLOUGHBY'S RETURN

JANE AUSTEN'S *SENSE AND SENSIBILITY* CONTINUES

JANE ODIWE

"A tale of almost irresistible temptation."

A lost love returns, rekindling forgotten passions…

When Marianne Dashwood marries Colonel Brandon, she puts her heartbreak over dashing scoundrel John Willoughby behind her. Three years later, Willoughby's return throws Marianne into a tizzy of painful memories and exquisite feelings of uncertainty. Willoughby is as charming, as roguish, and as much in love with her as ever. And the timing couldn't be worse—with Colonel Brandon away and Willoughby determined to win her back…

Praise for *Lydia Bennet's Story*:

"A breathtaking Regency romp!" —Diana Birchall, author of *Mrs. Darcy's Dilemma*

"An absolute delight."
—*Historical Novels Review*

"Odiwe emulates Austen's famous wit, and manages to give Lydia a happily-ever-after ending worthy of any Regency romance heroine." —*Booklist*

"Odiwe pays nice homage to Austen's stylings and endears the reader to the formerly secondary character, spoiled and impulsive Lydia Bennet."
—*Publishers Weekly*

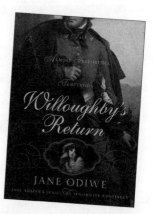

978-1-4022-2267-2
$14.99 US/$18.99 CAN/£7.99 UK

In the Arms of Mr. Darcy

SHARON LATHAN

If only everyone could be as happy as they are...

Darcy and Elizabeth are as much in love as ever—even more so as their relationship matures. Their passion inspires everyone around them, and as winter turns to spring, romance blossoms around them.

Confirmed bachelor Richard Fitzwilliam sets his sights on a seemingly unattainable, beautiful widow; Georgiana Darcy learns to flirt outrageously; the very flighty Kitty Bennet develops her first crush, and Caroline Bingley meets her match.

But the path of true love never does run smooth, and Elizabeth and Darcy are kept busy navigating their friends and loved ones through the inevitable separations, misunderstandings, misgivings, and lovers' quarrels to reach their own happily ever afters...

"If you love *Pride and Prejudice* sequels then this series should be on the top of your list!"
—*Royal Reviews*

"Sharon really knows how to make Regency come alive."
—*Love Romance Passion*

978-1-4022-3699-0
$14.99 US/$17.99 CAN/£9.99 UK

The Other Mr. Darcy

Pride and Prejudice continues...

Monica Fairview

"A lovely story… a joy to read."
—*Bookishly Attentive*

Unpredictable courtships appear to run in the Darcy family…

When Caroline Bingley collapses to the floor and sobs at Mr. Darcy's wedding, imagine her humiliation when she discovers that a stranger has witnessed her emotional display. Miss Bingley, understandably, resents this gentleman very much, even if he is Mr. Darcy's American cousin. Mr. Robert Darcy is as charming as Mr. Fitzwilliam Darcy is proud, and he is stunned to find a beautiful young woman weeping broken-heartedly at his cousin's wedding. Such depth of love, he thinks, is rare and precious. For him, it's love at first sight…

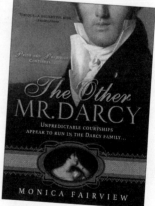

"An intriguing concept… a delightful ride in the park."
—*Austenprose*

978-1-4022-2513-0
$14.99 US/$18.99 CAN/£7.99 UK

Mr. Darcy Takes a Wife

LINDA BERDOLL
The #1 best-selling Pride and Prejudice *sequel*

"Wild, bawdy, and utterly enjoyable." *—Booklist*

Hold on to your bonnets!

Every woman wants to be Elizabeth Bennet Darcy—beautiful, gracious, universally admired, strong, daring and outspoken—a thoroughly modern woman in crinolines. And every woman will fall madly in love with Mr. Darcy—tall, dark and handsome, a nobleman and a heartthrob whose virility is matched only by his utter devotion to his wife. Their passion is consuming and idyllic—essentially, they can't keep their hands off each other—through a sweeping tale of adventure and misadventure, human folly and numerous mysteries of parentage. This sexy, epic, hilarious, poignant and romantic sequel to *Pride and Prejudice* goes far beyond Jane Austen.

What readers are saying:

"I couldn't put it down."

"I didn't want it to end!"

"Berdoll does Jane Austen proud!…A thoroughly delightful and engaging book."

"Delicious fun…I thoroughly enjoyed this book."

"My favorite *Pride and Prejudice* sequel so far."

978-1-4022-0273-5 • $16.95 US/ $19.99 CAN/ £9.99 UK